Attack

By Natalie Saar

ISBN 978-1-7378835-0-0

To mom,
The only person who could teach me prepositions
and who got me hooked on true crime.

1

Ella felt like the world was attacking her from every side. Though she couldn't see it, she sensed something was looming outside her front door, something else was watching her from the closet. Escape wasn't an option. Maybe if she sat very still the invisible threat wouldn't notice her and she'd be free.

In reality, nothing was happening. 29-year-old Ella was sitting on her bed, looking at a very normal credit card bill for $30, one that she paid every month. But every bill had the potential to trigger a mini panic attack.

The money to pay the bill wasn't an issue, it was all of the things that came *with* the bill that sent her spiraling. Thinking about those companies and the strangers working at those companies knowing where they could find Ella at any given time. The reality that while there was enough money right now, if she lost her job, there wasn't enough savings to keep paying the $30 bill on time *and* still afford to eat or buy gas. Then there was her car. It needed a repair; she wasn't sure what. All she knew was it made a grinding sound and she likely didn't have enough money for whatever was wrong with it.

After a couple of hard months during her last layoff, Ella missed some car payments and received some really odd calls. She later learned they were from a "repo man" trying to get her car. One time he called saying he had a FedEx package that she needed to meet him to sign for. That sounded odd, and made Ella worry that if she tried to pick up this package she'd be kidnapped by the guy. Frankly, she wondered if she should call FedEx and turn the guy in because he was making their company look creepy.

Ella never met him, but her personal world felt so exposed. Corners that she didn't know strangers could get to — like her exact home location at any time — were being invaded. After she finally got another job, which included an invasive background check, she caught up on her car payments, paid rent on time, and ate ramen for two weeks.

Only a month later, Ella's credit card was stolen. She called the credit card companies and did all of the right things to shut down her accounts and lock up her Social Security number. But she didn't realize she was too late. At a friend's wedding in a remote location, she got a call from someone saying that he was with the IRS and she'd missed a payment. If she didn't pay them right away, they were sending the sheriff to pick her up and haul her to jail.

So, Ella got another member of the wedding party to take her a bank where she sat in tense silence the whole time. The bank was closed for another two hours, and the hairstylist was waiting to do her hair back at the hotel. Ella called the IRS man back, and he told her that she could pay in iTunes cards and wire him the money.

At this point, Ella realized something was wrong. This is when Ella realized her SSN was stolen and these calls were part of her life now.

About once a month, someone called from a different organization, threatening to throw her in jail if she didn't pay them this or that.

And that's when Ella learned that people could find the address for not only her but her entire family just by Googling her name. So, that crazy ex who she contemplated serving a restraining order could be lurking outside her home at any moment. She immediately emailed the company asking them to hide her address, but they wouldn't without a $30 membership payment.

So, it would come down to paying this $30 credit card bill on time, or living every day knowing that her exact location, her sanctuary, her home, were on display for the world, and she was too broke to do anything about it.

Since the credit bureaus don't care about people's personal safety — she also had to pay them to shut down her SSN number after it was stolen. Ella logged on to the website and paid the $30 credit card bill.

2

It was Wednesday, which is why when Ella was called in to a meeting with her boss and 10 other colleagues, she didn't think anything of it. She worked for an entertainment magazine, which was much less exciting than it sounded. People usually assumed she hobnobbed with celebs all day and knew about movies well before they were announced to the public, but that wasn't the case. Far from it.

For Ella, a normal day consisted of getting up at 5am, assembling an outfit that was slightly nicer than a gym outfit, and heading to work by 6am. Over the last year, Ella had worked hard to get her 5'5" frame in shape. She went running most days of the week, and yoga most evenings. But the biggest benefit Ella found from this routine was that now it was easier to get dressed quickly in the morning. Everything fit the way she wanted it to, so even if the colors were a little off, somehow she still achieved the look of someone who had put in some effort that morning.

This Wednesdays was one of those days. Ella had overslept by 15 minutes, giving her exactly five minutes to get dressed, two minutes to brush her teeth, and five minutes to walk to her car down the street. She pulled on some black slim fit jeans, a white tank top, a black blazer, and a pair of ballet flats. But she broke her rule of not getting dressed before brushing her teeth, and inevitably got some toothpaste on her tank.

Digging through her clothes, Ella realized that was her last clean tank, so the blazer wouldn't work anymore. She reached for a sweater that wasn't the nicest, but if she swapped out her flats for a pair of black boots, she was put back together. Unfortunately, this outfit swap cost her valuable time and she was going to be late.

Nobody walked in Los Angeles which meant the apartments with parking spaces were pricey. So she frequently had to park several blocks away from where she lived.

She got to the office five minutes late and tried to get to her desk unnoticed. That's when she saw the last-minute meeting pop up on her calendar, scheduled for 6:30am. The early time probably should have given her some pause.

As soon as she'd poured herself a cup of coffee and cleared out the emails that had come in overnight, it was time to go to the meeting. No one really talked to each other before

7am, so the fact that everyone was glued to their laptops and phones seemed normal. It wasn't until Robert, the HR guy, walked in that people looked up and got a little concerned.

The meeting was prompt. Robert, a tall, handsome man in his early 50s with a full head of gray hair, was unusually serious. He explained that the magazine was making cuts, and the people in this room were the first to go. There would be boxes on their desks by the time they got back down there so they could pack up their things. Security would escort them out.

Ella was sipping her coffee, but at some point had stopped and looked around the room, seeing the same looks on everyone's faces that she likely had on her own. Robert kept talking but none of it really registered, and without knowing what she was doing, Ella said, "But it's a Wednesday."

That shut Robert up, and he now shared the same confused look as everyone else in the room, trying to figure out what she meant by that. "Well, it's just that... no one gets laid off on a Wednesday, do they? What kind of joke is this?"

No one said a word to her, but instead went right back to what they were doing. Some people left the room crying. Other managers tried to answer questions. Ella just sat there and glanced down at her phone that had an alert reminding her to make her car payment today. She swiped it away, chugged her coffee, stood up and walked back to her desk.

All around her, people were crying and hugging each other. The ones who weren't laid off seemed to be crying the most. It was called "survivor's remorse" Ella later learned. She didn't care about that or the things on her desk. The only thing she wondered was how she was going to find a job before rent was due in a couple of weeks.

3

The rest of that day was like a haze. Ella got to her car and immediately texted her friends group chat to tell them the news.

ELLA: Umm... I got laid off.
MINDY: OMG WHAT?! Tell us everything.
ZORA: Are you ok?
LULU: Again? Sux...
ELLA: Yeah, I'm fine. But if any of you know of any jobs, I could use one ASAP.

Ella locked her phone and headed to buy the two things she really needed right now: carbs and alcohol. She ran into the corner market for a couple packs of ramen, a shaker of parmesan cheese, some butter, and a couple bottles of "Two Buck Chuck." Desperate times called for desperately cheap measures. Her phone buzzed in her purse as she reached in to get her wallet. She used $6 in dimes and nickels to pay.

The cashier looked sadly at Ella as she counted out all of the change. Either that or she was looking sadly at this woman who was clearly planning to start drinking and eating cheap ramen at 7am. Either way, Ella hurriedly paid and left the store as fast as possible. She sat back down in her car, just noticing that her gas light had been on for a while, and headed for home, praying the gas lasted that long.

Ella lived on a sleepy street in Silverlake, in the east part of Los Angeles. It was one of the few places left where you could find rent at decent prices as long as you didn't let the parking situation drive you crazy. It was getting more hip, with lots of bands playing in the area, and a recent pop-up concert by the Rolling Stones who seemed to have done the show just because they were bored.

Today, there was a small blessing in her life though: a parking spot on her street. Ella pulled into it as fast as she could, obviously irritating a driver who had turned the corner right after her and now had to go hunting somewhere else. Though, now that she had this spot so close to her apartment, Ella started thinking that it would have been a good idea to pack up the box on her desk after all. She had some cute photos and a coffee mug she loved, even though she rarely ever used it for drinking. It was just a bright thing to look at on boring days.

Her phone continued buzzing, and Ella wished that she hadn't told the whole group and maybe had only mentioned it to Zora, but it was too late for that now. Besides, Mindy would have been pissed if she knew that Ella had told Zora first. It was always better to break big news to the group at the same time.

Ella locked her car, took a cautious look around the street for any shady folks, then walked up to her apartment. She grabbed a small cooking pot from the cupboard above her stove, filled it with water, and turned on the burner. While she waited for it to boil, she caught up with some of the messages.

ZORA: I'll ask around. Worse comes to worse, you can always go back to the studio.

"The studio" was the yoga studio where Zora and Ella met years ago. Ella was new to Los Angeles, but not new to yoga which was having a renaissance in this image-obsessed city. So she got a job at the front desk of a local studio, which is where she met not only Zora, but also the manager of the magazine from which she'd just been let go.

Zora was the type of woman who other women can't stop staring at. She was a lithe 5'8" with the shade of dark golden skin that made everyone ask what nationality she was. Even though she was only in her early 30s, Zora had her shit together. She was the type of person that made you want to step your game up.

MINDY: You know I've got you if you need some cash. Just say the word!

Mindy was Ella's best childhood friend. They'd grown up in Arizona but moved to Los Angeles to go to UCLA. Even though they both got into USC too, Mindy had decided they'd go to UCLA because blue looked good on her. At nearly six feet tall with blonde hair and icy blue eyes, Mindy had no problem getting modeling jobs in LA. Though, when Mindy showed up places with Ella, people were always a little confused about if Ella was her assistant or what.

It also helped Mindy's image when people found out her family was filthy rich.

LULU: Oh em gee Mins! You are so nice!

Lulu was a smaller, slightly duller clone of Mindy and did everything in her power to let people know she was Mindy's best friend. They rushed the same sorority together, and from the first day, Lulu decided that Mindy was the best thing since cauliflower pizza crust. Lulu and Ella got along fine but they had nothing in common except Mindy, who made sure Lulu was included in all of their group activities.

Knowing this made Ella pause from time to time before she opened up an activity or topic to the rest of the group. Sometimes she just texted Zora instead.

TRIX: You can always come work with me. ;)

Ella was shocked that Trix was awake this early and could only assume that she was in fact just still up from the night before. Trix was in her late 20s and also met Ella and Zora at an exercise class, but it wasn't yoga.

At night, Trix was a stripper at one of the hottest clubs on the Sunset Strip. She actually had a pretty big fandom because she wasn't your average stripper. Barely 5'0", Trix was curvy in all of the right places. She was half Thai, which she said is where she got her jet-black hair from, even though it was curly, which she attributed to her Jamaican mother.

During the day, afternoon, and sometimes nights if she wasn't at the club, Trix taught pole dancing aerobics classes which were a surprisingly hard work out. Ella wasn't sure which of those jobs Trix was talking about, but she wasn't in a position to be choosy if some prospects didn't turn up right now.

The water in the pot had begun boiling, and Ella tossed in a palette of ramen. She stirred it with a fork for a couple minutes before draining it and tossing in some butter, parmesan cheese sprinkles, and garlic powder. It was about as unhealthy as food could get.

MINDY: Ok, emergency happy hour today. I'm buying and everyone is coming.
TRIX: I'm not coming. But you have my support.
ELLA: I'm in no position to pass up free drinks. I'll be there.
LULU: Um DUH! I'm totally there. Great idea!
ZORA: I may be a little late, but count me in.

Ella slurped up her ramen, sat down at her desk and started applying to any and all jobs that she was remotely qualified for.

4

Mindy found a happy hour near Ella so that Ella could drink and not have to pay for an Uber home. It was unusually considerate of Mindy, Ella thought to herself when Mindy suggested the meetup. Of course, coming to the east side of town meant that Trix would not even consider getting in rush hour traffic to join, and Ella assumed that was part of the reason Mindy had suggested it.

TRIX: Have fun! Next time drinks are on me.

Everyone knew she didn't mean it though. Trix had no shortage of cash, but she had a shortage of stability, so every extra dollar either went into her savings account or elsewhere in her budget.

Ella was the first to arrive at the darkly lit bar that had a Buddha painted on the outside of it. She sat down at a table and texted everyone that she had a spot in the back. They slowly trickled in. Mindy was there first, with Lulu only minutes behind. Then Zora walked in about 30 minutes after. By Los Angeles standards though, they were all relatively on time.

"Ok, now that we're all here, tell us everything, El," Mindy announced to the group instead of asking Ella.

"Well, I guess I should have seen it coming because it was weird to schedule a meeting that early in the morning—"

"Yeah, but it was a Wednesday," Zora said, cutting her off.

"That's what I said!" It was one of those moments when it was clear to Ella why these were her friends.

"Ok keep going," Mindy urged her.

"Well, that's basically it. We signed some papers and had boxes on our desks, but I left mine and I just walked out."

"But what about that cute pencil set I got you last Christmas?" Lulu asked.

Ella had no idea what she was talking about but played it off. "Oh, I have that set at home. It was way too chic for work."

"Oh, true!" Lulu said as she sat back, delighted by that answer.

The server walked up to the table with a tray of drinks. Ella was a vodka soda girl, while Zora was more of a whiskey person. Mindy liked to think that her signature drink was a tequila soda, but it was really whatever she felt like that day, and Lulu got whatever Mindy was having.

"Cheers," Mindy said, raising her glass. "To new beginnings." They clinked glasses.

"The universe always has a way of pushing us into new and better things," Zora chimed in. She tended to have a positive yet realistic view on life. "Speaking of which, I may have a job lead for you."

Ella was shocked. She knew her friends said they'd ask around, but she figured it would take a few days for anyone to get back to them. Regardless, she was thrilled at the prospect of not filling out another application after spending the majority of her day trawling through job boards. She'd forgotten how tedious and time consuming they were. Even with a few versions of a general resume for slightly different jobs, it seemed to take about 30 minutes on average to fill out an application. It was basically a full-time job in itself.

"Oh my God! That's amazing! What is it?" Mindy exclaimed.

"Well, you'd be working with me for starters," Zora smiled and continued. Ella's face fell a little. She tried so hard not to let it but could feel it happening anyway. Working with Zora would be amazing, that wasn't the problem. It was where she worked that was the issue.

To hear Zora talk about it, she worked at one of the foremost companies when it came to the frontier of female empowerment and taking their bodies back from men. But to ask any outside the company, they'd tell you that they manufactured sex toys.

"Hey, hear me out," Zora said, noticing Ella's change in expression.

"Whatever it is, it's great, I'm sure! I'm really thankful you found something so fast," Ella tried to save herself, but wasn't sure if it worked.

"You'd be doing social media for all of our channels. It's actually a pretty easy job. People tell you what to post and you just hit send," Zora said.

"That's not too bad," Ella willing herself to warm up to the idea of hawking dildos.

"Not too bad? That sounds like a dream!" Mindy said, with Lulu nodding in agreement and sipping from the straw in her drink.

"So what's next? What do you need from me?" Ella asked Zora.

"Ladies, let's talk shop later. It sounds like we've found a place for our little Ella to land on her feet for now, so let's discuss something more fun, shall we?" Mindy said. Ella and Zora quickly rolled their eyes but caught each other's expressions. Zora mouthed, "I'll tell you later."

"I agree! What did you have in mind, Mindy?" Lulu asked.

"Well, I wanted to talk about our next book club. It's at my place, and it's going to be a special one. I can't tell you why yet, but be ready for the shock of a lifetime!" Mindy said as she raised her glass to herself and her secret news.

"More shocking than getting fired on a Wednesday?" Ella asked as a halfhearted joke.

"Honey, you weren't fired, you were laid off," said Mindy.

"Same difference," Ella shrugged.

"It's actually a very big difference to the unemployment office," Zora chimed in and Mindy gave a knowing nod.

"Really?" Ella asked.

"If they don't believe that you were laid off, then you might not get unemployment. You've filed for it already, right?" Mindy asked.

"No not... not yet. I was kind of hoping I'd get a job before it was necessary," Ella sheepishly answered.

"Better get on that, sweetie," Lulu said while slurping up the last of her cocktail. She took any opportunity to make Ella look bad and try to drive a wedge through Ella's and Mindy's friendship.

Once happy hour ended, Mindy picked up the tab and they all went their separate ways. But Zora walked Ella home to make sure she got there safely after her four drinks.

"So, how do I get this job?" Ella asked as they were walking.

"It's basically yours. You still have to fill out the application, but we're a small company so they take recommendations seriously. I'll email it to you when I get home. If you fill it out by tomorrow, you should be approved in time to start on Monday."

It may have been the alcohol, or the relief of a terrible day coming to a hopeful end, but Ella threw herself at Zora in the type of hug that Zora had to physically extricate herself from.

Tomorrow was a new day, and Ella was feeling pure gratitude and hope, and maybe a little bit drunk too.

5

Ella tried to let herself sleep in, but her brain had barely turned itself off long enough to get any sleep at all. As the sun peeked into her window, she rolled to the side of her bed and pulled her laptop out from underneath it.

Every day, Ella told herself that she was going to stop looking at a screen first thing in the morning, but every morning she woke up with some nagging thought that made her either reach for her phone or her computer. Each time she did, she promised herself that tomorrow would be the day she finally got up slowly, doing some yoga and meditating before engaging with the world. She knew that was a lie.

But today there was a good reason to start right away: she had to fill out her job application, which felt like something that could help her life just as much as a meditation sesh.

Ella opened the email attachment, which was of course a PDF. She had no printer or scanner. Why couldn't companies make everything electronic? It was 2020 after all. This meant she was going to have to go to Staples to print out the application, spend 30 minutes filling it out by hand, then scanning it and emailing it back. It was a hassle but the main thing blocking Ella now was that Staples didn't open for two more hours.

Her motivation to take on the day instantly died.

Putting down the computer, Ella stared at her ceiling wondering what she would do today. She could make ambitious plans like finally Marie Kondo-ing her apartment, but that felt aggressive. It was the type of day when she wished she had a boyfriend who could call out sick and they could spend all day together. But ever since breaking up with her ex, Chad, Ella had been hesitant to get back into dating. She had been so sure he was a good guy, not like everyone else.

When Ella and Chad had met, there was an immediate spark. They were at one of Mindy's parties, and he was hanging out by the patio. Ella had seen him as soon as he'd walked in but didn't want to seem too interested. He was your typical LA guy, but taller than most. Great hair, great smile, great style and an impossible perpetual 5 o'clock shadow; there was nothing she'd change about him physically. So of course his personality sucked, Ella guessed at the time, but she had to find out for herself.

The absolute opposite was true. Chad was smart, charming, funny, and their conversation continued until the party emptied out and Mindy had to urge them to go home. Ella wondered if she should invite him over, but he took the lead.

"It was great talking. I'd like to do it again sometime. Here's my number," he said, writing it down on a napkin. So old school.

Ella didn't know how to respond. He wasn't trying to get in her pants, but he wanted to see her again. And he gave her all of the power by giving her *his* number, not asking for hers. His rideshare pulled up to the curb and he left.

They went out a few times after that, and Ella was more and more enchanted with Chad each time. Each date was different from any date she'd been on before. They were having experiences together, not only going to dinner. The first date was at the Santa Monica Pier where they rode the ferris wheel, he won her some carnival toys, and shared a funnel cake. A classic, sweet night. Then they went their separate ways.

The second date was at the Griffith Park Observatory. This time he'd offered to pick her up at her apartment because, according to Chad, parking was a nightmare at the top of the hill. Ella thought he was being sarcastic because parking anywhere in LA was a nightmare. When they got there, she saw how right he'd been; it was a parking nightmare unlike any she'd seen in the city. By some miracle they found a spot close to the observatory and got to see the stars and a killer view of the city. When Chad dropped her off, he gave her a sweet kiss, nothing too hot, and waited until she got inside her building before driving away.

For the third date, they went to a cooking class, making a gourmet pasta dinner for two. Tonight's the night, Ella had thought to herself, and she wasn't wrong. It was the night that would change the rest of her life.

6

Chad and Ella took their dinner back to Chad's place to enjoy it with some nice red wine. Everything was perfect. The food, the music, the way he asked her to dance even though they were the only two in the room. But right when Ella thought they were making their way toward the bedroom, Chad stopped her and said he wasn't ready yet, that he was still enjoying getting to know her.

Ella didn't realize what a trap this was. Most of her new relationships got physical and they spent less time talking after that, but Chad was the opposite. He wanted to know everything about her, even down to what her favorite toy was as a kid. They talked for hours and never ran out of things to say. She'd later learn that was her downfall.

As time went on, they eventually had sex, and it was great, nothing mind blowing, but good enough. It was clear that Chad was thinking through everything he was doing in bed which Ella thought took a bit of the fun out of it, but if that was the worst of their problems, she could handle it.

Then Chad started getting possessive. She'd caught him looking through her phone a few times. He said he just liked scrolling through her selfies because they were so cute, but she knew that he'd been snooping around. One time she'd playfully said that she gets to see his phone if he can see hers. He handed his over without hesitation.

Ella was shocked by how little was in his phone. Only a few numbers of people, some pictures of them together, and that was basically it. "Why do you even have a smartphone if you don't take advantage of it?" she'd asked.

"That's a good question," he answered with a wry smile. "Maybe I'll trade it in for an old school flip phone."

But then Chad started doing other weird things.

Ella caught him texting her friends as though he was her. When she questioned him, he'd say that he noticed the message and since she was busy, he wanted to help her out by making sure she didn't have to keep track of what she needed to reply to. She'd seen him waiting around her office at lunch. He said he wanted to surprise her, but he'd been the one who looked surprised when she approached him.

They'd bonded over the fact that both of them had lost their parents — his to cancer and hers to a car accident — but then that bond became odd. Chad would frequently tell Ella that she was all that he had, and that he didn't know what he'd do without her.

Chad was great, and things were great with him, but Ella didn't feel as strongly as he did. Chad kept assuring her that love took a while to grow and in time she'd feel the same way about him. But time went on and… she didn't.

Just before their one-year anniversary Ella decided to break things off. It seemed sensible since after a year of dating, she wasn't even close to in love with Chad, and he was just as clingy as ever. At dinner that night she planned to tell him.

"Chad, I have something to tell you."

"And I have something to *ask* you," he cut her off, smiling.

Oh no, Ella thought to herself. Whatever question he had, she was sure her answer would disappoint him.

"Ok, well, how about I go first since I said it first," she tried to be coy and stave off any embarrassment he might cause himself.

"Does yours come with a gift? Whoever gives a gift gets to go first," he rebuffed, still beaming.

"Ok fine, you go first," she said, deflated.

Chad reached into his pocket and pulled out a small black velvet box. He can't possibly be proposing, Ella thought. She tried to stop him, but he opened the box too quickly. Inside, Ella was relieved to find not a ring but a key. She sighed and couldn't help but smile, which gave him the wrong impression.

"Ella, I want you to move in with me," he looked the happiest Ella had ever seen him...

Taking the box and closing the lid, Ella took a deep breath. "I wish you'd have let me go first," she said.

Chad sat back, looking confused. Ella continued, "I think we need to break up."

The conversation that ensued was ugly. Chad cried… a lot. He tried saying everything to make her change her mind and she almost did if only to stop him being so sad. But she knew breaking up was the right choice and she'd have to stand firm.

In the weeks that followed, Chad would not leave her alone. He kept popping up at all of her regular places. The coffee shop she stopped at in the mornings, the happy hour bar she met her friends at, the gym. But he never approached her, he just watched her. She could feel his eyes on her all of the time, and never quite felt safe again. She used to leave her windows open at home but not anymore. She changed her routine, asked her job for different hours, but she couldn't shake him.

After a while, Ella decided something more drastic was necessary and she served him a restraining order. That seemed to do the trick because Ella never saw him again, but she always felt that he was still there, watching her from behind every corner.

7

Ella hadn't dated much since Chad, and her friends were always telling her it was time to put herself out there again. So, since she had nothing but time and no will to get out of bed, she decided to take the leap and download a dating app.

Even though she wasn't particularly sold on dating anyone right now — she was kind of a mess, truth be told — Ella knew her friends were right. The only way to shake the feeling that Chad was always lurking around each corner was to move on.

The amount of dating apps to choose from was shocking. There was something for people who wanted to hook up, people who were interested in meditation, people who were Christian farmers, people in the LGBTQ+ community, people who wanted to date seriously but not that seriously, people who really seriously wanted to date. The options were so overwhelming that she almost gave up, but she didn't. She stayed focused on her goal: find a dating app. She settled on the second to last, an app for people who wanted to date seriously but not that seriously; she was just trying to get back in the saddle again after all.

The task of writing a bio and picking a profile picture was also harder than Ella had anticipated. Should she use the pic she uploaded for social media sites or the one she used for her more professional sites? She went with one that hadn't been used anywhere. It was from a day out at the wineries with her friends where she looked casual, fun, relaxed, and approachable. As for the bio... that was a little more difficult.

"29-year-old social media manager who loves to work hard and play hard."

No, that sounds corny, she thought to herself. Besides, should she even put how old she is?

"Loves a good glass of wine and a laugh. Looking for someone who can give her both."

That was even worse than the first one, she chided herself.

Ella went through several more mental attempts before she settled on one, for now, more out of exhaustion than satisfaction.

"Enjoying life and looking for someone who she can share it with."

Short, simple, not revealing, and to the point.

Ella looked at the clock. She was shocked to see that all of this had taken an hour to put together. She hopped out of bed, made some coffee, got dressed, and headed to Staples to print out her application.

8

Ella was early and the store wasn't open yet. She didn't mind though; at least she'd gotten up and out of the house. She knew from past experience that the longer she moped around, the more time her anxiety had to creep in. If she could keep busy, then she'd be able to outrun it for as long as possible.

So rather than worry about if this job would really pan out, or if she'd have enough money to pay rent in a couple of weeks, or any other thought that was seeping into her consciousness, Ella pulled out her phone and opened her dating app. There were no notifications or anything, so she checked the settings to make sure her profile was published. It was. She briefly talked herself down from the "I'm hideous and no one will ever love me" ledge and began looking at the profiles of the men on there.

Kevin, 32, actor/bartender. Dog daddy, world traveler, love being in love.

Nope.

Latrell, 29, investment banker. Living life one day at a time.

Maybe.

Joe, 21, waiter, Work all day, party all night. Limo buses are my jam.

No. So much no.

Waleed, 30, marketing manager, trying to be a better man every day. Looking for someone to go on this journey with.

Hmm, ok.

Then she saw him.

Chad, 35, entrepreneur, nice guy looking for a nice girl who won't break my heart.

Isn't that a little pathetic, Ella thought to herself? Not only was he not over her, but he was making sure everyone else knew about it too. But she couldn't help herself and got curious. She clicked on his profile.

If she thought he was pathetic before, the pictures only reaffirmed that. Over half of them were pictures they'd taken together that he'd cropped her out of. In one, he'd photoshopped her face out, leaving only her body, and captioned it, "This could be us, but you haven't swiped."

Ella was so involved in looking at Chad's profile that once again she lost track of time. There were no in-depth details, but she was looking for anything that would give her an indication that he was still the psycho she thought he'd been. She couldn't find anything though.

Just then, there was a loud knocking at her car window, and Ella jumped, letting out a little shocked yelp, and dropping her phone. She looked over to see... Chad?! No, never mind, it wasn't Chad, it was just the security guard and her imagination playing tricks on her.

"Yes?" She rolled down her window a little.

"Are you here to go to Staples?" he asked. He looked a lot like Chad if she was being honest with herself.

"Uh, yes. I'm just waiting for it to open."

"Ok, well it's open now, so you can either go in, or I'm going to have to ask you to leave the parking lot."

"Oh, ok thank you," she said, rolling up her windows and gathering her things. She reached over to pick her phone up off the floor, realizing her screen hadn't locked and Chad's profile was gone. She'd accidentally swiped right, which meant he'd get a notification.

Ella panicked, not wanting him to contact her or even know that she was looking at his profile. How had she been so stupid? And why did she spend so much time trying to look into his life? She hadn't wanted to be a part of it so why did she let curiosity get the best of her?

Not knowing what to do, Ella deactivated her account and deleted the app from her phone, praying that he hadn't already seen the notification. She'd blocked his number and email in the past, but double checked just to make sure they were still blocked.

Slightly shaking and not sure what else she could do, Ella grabbed her purse and walked inside.

9

Ella printed out her application and halfway through it realized she had no idea what Zora's current job was at the company. She seemed to like it though, and that was good enough for Ella.

Staples was vacant except for her and a few workers, so she took her time filling out her application. And she remembered she still had to tell the group about what had happened with the dating app.

ELLA: Omg, you guys, I just did the stupidest thing.
MINDY: What was it?!?
LULU: Yeah! Tell us!

Anytime Ella had something slightly embarrassing to tell everyone she always wished there was a separate chat without Lulu in it, but Mindy had made her part of the group, so she had to deal with it.

ELLA: I had a couple of hours to kill today, and I downloaded a dating app.
ZORA: Woah

ELLA: I know. So anyways, I didn't see anyone who looked promising, and then you won't believe who I saw...

TRIX: Keanu Reeves

ELLA: What? No, why would Keanu Reeves be on there? I saw Chad!

MINDY: Oh no...

ELLA: Yeah, exactly. Then when the security guard startled me in my car while I was looking at his profile, I dropped my phone and swiped on him by accident.

ZORA: Biiiiiiiiiitch

ELLA: I know, I know. So, I deleted it immediately, but do you think he got a notification or saw it? Freaking out a little bit.

Ella was freaking out a lot but only Zora would understand that. Everyone else would think she was being dramatic.

MINDY: I'm sure it's fine. It's not like he was holding his phone when it happened.

LULU: Unless he was, then he definitely saw it.

Ella regretted texting the group. She should have just picked up the phone and called Zora. But it was too late now. She just had to play it off and get on with her day.

ELLA: Yeah, he probably didn't see it. Thanks for making me feel better!

Ella locked her phone, tossed it in her purse, and finished filling out the application uninterrupted. Another reason she hated applications was because she had so many jobs that she had to list and never knew the addresses or numbers without having to Google them.

After what felt like an hour later, she was done with the application and was ready to scan and email it to Zora, but she texted her first.

ELLA: Should I send this app to your work email? What is it?
ZORA: Yup. zora@funinbed.com
ELLA: Wait... that's your work email?
ZORA: Yeah, it's the name of the company. Didn't you read the application?

Ella had in fact not thoroughly read the application. She was only looking at the blank spaces that needed to be filled in, checked vacant check boxes, and signed the empty signature lines. But Zora didn't need to know all of that.

ELLA: Oh, right, yeah totally.

ZORA: You didn't read it...

ELLA: I just need a job. I don't care what it is.

ZORA: Well, it won't be long now. Just send it over and I'll forward it to HR. When can you start?

ELLA: This afternoon lol

ZORA: Ok well it'll probably be more like next week, but good to know.

ELLA: Thanks, Zor. Let me know if you need anything else!

Zora texted back a thumbs up emoji and Ella hit send on the email.

It wasn't even noon and it had already been a rollercoaster of a day, but it was starting to look up. Ella decided to go home, treat herself to a pint of mint chip Halo Top ice cream, and binge watch Netflix.

10

To Ella's great relief, all of the paperwork went through just fine, but she'd had no idea what she'd really signed up for until she got to work that Monday. Zora was in a meeting during the time Ella was told to arrive for orientation, so she made her way to the reception desk to check in.

A lithe woman was at the desk. Her appearance made it hard to distinguish what nationality she was, which intrigued Ella. She was tan, but the shade of tan that could be either natural or a result of attending weekend rooftop pool parties. She wore her dark hair in a bun and had black eyes that were somehow still very bright and welcoming. In short, she was gorgeous.

"Hi, I'm Ella and it's my first day. They told me to chec–"

"Ella! Hi!" She said, surprising Ella by hopping out of her seat and grabbing some papers in one motion. She came out from around the back of the desk. "I'm Marley. Zora told me all about you! I'll show you around and take you to your seat."

Once they stepped past the reception desk, Ella was hit with the realization she had no idea exactly what she'd signed up for here.

There were dildos everywhere she looked.

The first thing that caught Ella's eye was a giant two-story cartoon mural of a pink dildo and something that looked like a lavender colored labia. She couldn't figure out how, but in some way these items looked *cute* like in a teddy bear way that made her want both of them immediately.

Marley saw Ella mesmerized and laughed as though this happens all of the time. "Don't you worry," she said in a friendly tone, "You've got a welcome pack waiting on your desk for you," and winked at Ella.

"Oh! Ha– Thanks," she nervously laugh-talked.

"Just a little further to go," Marley said, but Ella was barely listening. It was like an adorable sex part factory in here. She thought that she was relatively adventurous in bed, had even used handcuffs once, but now she was questioning all of that. She was glad that it seemed like everything here was clearly meant to be aesthetically pleasing though, not like those horrible realistic dildos she'd seen in her friends' rooms before.

Everything here could be just as welcome as a bachelorette party as it could at a women's book club, albeit an edgy book club. The more she looked around, the more Ella realized this job was going to be a lot of fun. Not only for her personally, but for her creatively. She was going to be able to socialize these products in a way that made people want them without the items being too overt or offensive.

Marley abruptly stopped in front of her, and Ella nearly ran into her. "Here's your desk!" Marley said cheerfully.

"Thanks," Ella said, trying to mimic Marley's tone but knowing she failed.

"Don't worry, you'll get used to it all soon enough," Marley said, patting her on the back. "Ok, back to the front desk for me. Anything else you need right now, El?"

Ella didn't like it when people who had just met her started using nicknames, but there was something about Marley that made Ella feel like she'd actually be offended if Marley used her full name, like maybe she wasn't cool or something.

"Actually, yeah one more thing. Do you know where Zora sits? She's my best fri—"

"Oh my God! You know Zora? She's one of my faves. Sometimes she reads my tarot for me and it's always scary-true. She sits on the other side of the building, and it's a little tricky getting there. How about I ping her and tell her to swing on by?"

"Yeah, that would be great. Thanks!" Ella said, still trying to sound as excited as Marley which felt incredibly unnatural.

"Great! Ok, your computer is right there on your desk with all of your instructions. Your manager is OOO today, but she said that she sent some emails your way. Besides, the first day is usually just a lot of administrative and tech stuff anyway," Marley quickly explained. "Ping me if you need anything," she yelled while walking away.

Ella sat down at her desk, looking at her shiny new MacBook which was hooked up to a bigger monitor. They all sat in cubicles that had low walls, so it was a mix of a cubicle and an open floor plan. No one else was sitting in her area, but Ella figured they'd come in later. Afterall, this didn't strike her as the type of place where people came to work early.

While she waited for Zora, Ella let the reality of this job sink in, realizing that it was now a part of her resume, a part of her professional history. This was hardly a professional place, but then again, it was a business, and from all appearances it was a business that was very successful.

But no matter how hard she tried, the anxiety of knowing that she'd have to talk to any future employer about working for a sex toy company was creating a wave of anxiety that she was trying to keep from cresting. No matter how many times she thought about how she'd try and explain that they were cute sex toys, it wouldn't go over well.

Then again, she thought to herself, porn stars eventually find work after their careers are over, right? So, this had to be easier than that, *right*?

11

Ella was in the midst of filling out seemingly endless new hire paperwork when Zora came up behind her and made her jump.

"Oh my God! You scared me!" Ella laughed.

"Good; then my plan worked," Zora smiled back, hugging Ella. "So how are you settling in?"

"Um, you never told me that *this* is where you worked. Do you think there's enough dicks?"

"Hey, did you want a job or not?"

Ella sighed, knowing Zora was right. She couldn't have survived missing more than one paycheck. And deep down she knew she was really grateful to be out of her house and feeling useful again.

"Ok, ok. So why don't you show me around."

"Right this way," Zora said, waving Ella down a hall she hadn't explored yet. "I'll show you my desk first, so you can find me if you need anything." They walked past so many phalluses that even only an hour into working here, Ella was numb to seeing them. Different parts of the building were dedicated to different departments, but the only department Ella was really interested in was the kitchen. There were more snacks there than she'd ever seen, and Zora said that on Fridays, they did an open bar office happy hour there around 3pm. It was their sneaky way of getting people to come in on Fridays and to work a little later.

Eventually they made it to Zora's desk, which of course was on the complete opposite side of the building from Ella. Then, a very surreal moment happened that made Ella question whether or not this was real life.

As they got closer, the most handsome man Ella had ever seen stood up from the desk next to Zora. He saw the two women and flashed a smile so sparkling and genuine that Ella had to steady herself. He was tall, at least 6'3" and had one of those rare, perfect bodies that was somehow made for a t-shirt and jeans. Ella pulled her gaze back up to his face which was so beautiful it was almost hard to look at. His cheekbones were chiseled in a way that naturally drew her to look at his full lips which were wrapped around the most brilliant white smile. His dark brown hair was floppy yet somehow still styled, and Ella had no idea how that was possible. It was like someone ripped him from a Dolce & Gabbana ad but then somehow improved on it.

"Zora! Back so soon?" he joked, running a hand through his hair.

"Yeah, I tried to stretch out the tour, but this one walks fast," Zora effortlessly joked back, and Ella had no idea how Zora was even able to keep cool around him.

"And who is this fast walker?" he asked.

"Oh, right. This is my friend Ella. Today's her first day here."

"Nice to meet you Ella," he said, extending his hand. "I'm Jake."

"Yes, you are," Ella said, because those happened to be the first words that escaped from her mouth, and she instantly wanted to put them back in.

Jake chuckled. "You're funny," he said, and Ella tried to giggle but it turned into an awful mix of a laugh and a gasp. She was, unable to look away from him, and apparently unable to stop shaking his strong hand which almost fully enveloped hers. "And I see you like shaking hands?" he half joked.

Ella was mortified and snatched her hand back. "I'm so sorry –" she started to say but Zora cut her off.

"She's just not used to seeing someone as good looking as you," Zora said coolly, without a hint of humor in her voice. It clearly made Jake a little uncomfortable.

"Ahh c'mon Z. I'm not *that* good looking." Ella thought she saw him blushing when he said it.

"Bull*shit*. I don't even like guys, and I'd consider switching teams for the night," Zora said and winked. Jake laughed.

"Ok, well I'll see you two later. Maybe we can grab a drink after work or something," he said, continuing to walk off to wherever it was he'd gotten up to go to in the first place.

"You ok? I've never heard you make that sound before" Zora asked Ella after Jake walked off.

.

"What is wrong with you! How could you say that to him?!" Ella whisper-yelled at Zora, who started laughing so loud that someone looked over at them. Ella was mortified.

"Chill out, it's *fine*. He's just a guy, El."

"That's not even a human person. He's like a Greek statue that came to life and put on some clothes."

"I bet you wish he was naked like a statue, huh?" Zora joked, which made Ella gasp and hold her breath, until she eventually nodded and exhaled.

"Ok, just give me a freaking second to get my brain back together."

Ella sat there, staring straight ahead trying to think about anything except Jake's bone structure, but the only things around to distract her were cotton candy colored silicone penises, so it was a lost cause.

"Let's go to lunch," Zora said with a smile, seeing that her friend was obviously struggling to get a grip.

Ella was still staring straight ahead, so Zora playfully hugged her from behind, pulling Ella up to a standing position, and guiding her back the direction they came from.

A million thoughts were running through Ella's head, not the least of which was why a guy like that was working at a place like this. Was he a sex addict? Then again, he could be wondering the same about her. Maybe he was just a guy who needed a job and ended up staying. That's the story Ella decided she would tell herself. Of course, she could ask Zora and find out the truth, but for now she wanted to let herself believe this fan fic she'd made up.

12

Now that Ella knew what she was walking into, her second day was much better than her first. She waved at Marley on the way in and plopped down at her desk, ready to get to work. Her boss was still out of town, so she spent some time going through their team documents on their cloud drive.

The amount of faux dicks she was around was truly so overwhelming that she got used to them in under a day. They were just part of the aesthetic. The more Ella looked around at them, the more she realized how purposefully the place had been decorated and wondered for a second if she actually liked the style here?

Ella had tried to put off thinking about Jake sitting just one floor above her for as long as she could, but that was impossible. She hadn't been able to stop thinking about him since the moment she'd walked away from him. There were a few moments here and there where she thought about work or what she was going to eat for her next meal, but then sure enough, that chiseled face with its perfect bone structure popped back into her mind.

And now in this moment, Ella realized she was just staring at her screen, thinking about Jake, so she got up to make the trek to the kitchen and get some coffee. She was still trying to get her bearings around the labyrinthian offices but was able to navigate her way after a few wrong turns.

She hadn't actually made any coffee yesterday, and now that the machine was sitting in front of her, Ella realized she had no idea how to work this industrial-sized thing. She found a button on the screen that looked like it was a cup of black coffee, not a latte or a cappuccino or anything. Then she found the button for iced, not hot. Then she pushed "Start" realizing too late that she'd forgotten to put a cup under the dispenser where a strong, steady stream of coffee was shooting straight down, making a mess on the floor and splattering onto her meticulously chosen Day Two outfit.

Ella scrambled to find a cup and napkins, but her brain wasn't working fast enough and she tried to reach for both, grabbing neither, and letting a stack of cups and napkins fall to the ground. Exasperated, she finally got a cup and caught the rest of the coffee stream right as it was finishing, then set about cleaning up the mess on the floor when she heard a laugh from behind her.

"So, I guess Z didn't teach you how to use the coffee machine then?" a man's voice said, and Ella didn't even need to look to know it was Jake. She tried to act as cool and nonchalant as possible as she slowly stood up, holding a napkin dripping in coffee.

"No, I guess she didn't," Ella nervously smiled and gave a halfhearted laugh.

"Let me help you clean that up, and then I'll show you how to work this thing. Don't worry, this happens to a lot of people on their first try," Jake said, making his way over to her, and squatting down on the floor with napkins in his hand.

"Did you make a mess like this?" Ella asked, hoping she'd find some flaw in him.

"No, but I usually read directions," he joked. It should have sounded conceited coming from someone who looked like him, but somehow it didn't.

The cleanup didn't take long with two people. They stood up, washed their hands, and Jake reached for a clean cup. "Now, let's try this again."

Of course, everything went perfectly and Ella's iced coffee was streaming into her cup without a hitch. She wanted to say something to fill the awkward time while the cup was filling, but Jake had an air about him that made her think he couldn't even understand what an awkward feeling was. He was the one to break the silence.

"So, we didn't get to go out for that drink with Z last night. What do you think about you and I going to the brewery down the street for happy hour?" he asked.

Ella was shocked at how easily he'd asked her out that she wasn't even sure he had. She tried to say yes, but accidentally inhaled, catching a gulp of air in her mouth when she meant to say yes, so she just made an odd noise and nodded. He laughed an easy laugh and handed her the now-full coffee.

"Great. I'll swing by your desk at 5 then. Try not to make too many other messes today," he winked and walked away.

13

It had been a surprisingly busy day for someone who didn't know exactly what it was that she was supposed to be doing yet. Ella read all of the brand guidelines and looked at their social media strategy up to this point, but she figured they brought her in because they wanted some kind of positive change in engagement, and she was going to help them get it.

Emails trickled in throughout the day with requests for upcoming campaign copy and she did her best, all the while taking notes about how she was going to improve upon what they had right now. Toward the end of the day, the requests stopped coming in and she was in the middle of putting together a presentation evaluating the directions they could take with their channels.

Their Twitter wasn't as interactive as the big hitters like Moon Pie and Wendy's which it definitely should be since they were promoting such a fun product. They weren't working with enough influencers on Instagram, and Ella had a few ideas to tie in their products with a few Real Housewives personalities. She thought that Lisa Rinna and

Erika Jayne in particular would be good choices to help shill their stock.

Right when she was in the middle of photoshopping what a potential partnership ad would look like, someone tapped Ella's shoulder, making her nearly jump out of her chair. It was Jake standing there smiling at her.

"Sorry, didn't mean to scare you," he casually laughed. "I tried to get your attention, but you were so focused with your headphones on. Ready to take a break and get some drinks?"

"It is time already?!" Ella couldn't believe it but after spending her morning trying to think about anything except drinks later, she'd finally done it and totally lost track of time. "Sure, let me get my things together."

Ella was one of those people who carried her whole life in her purse, which was usually fine until someone had to watch you pull yourself together in just a few minutes. That's when it got embarrassing. So, she kept the gathering to a minimum, knowing she'd inevitably forget something anyway, and said, "Ok, ready! Where are we going?"

Jake led her out of the office, waving at Marley on the way, and made small talk about the brewery they were going to. But all that Ella could think about was what she may have forgotten that she'd like to have had a few moments to refresh her makeup, and then she realized he'd asked her a question.

"Sorry, I missed that. What did you say?" she sheepishly asked, realizing she hadn't even caught enough to fake an answer. He didn't look hurt, but more so inquiring about where her mind was at.

"We can reschedule if you have to get to some other stuff," he offered but didn't stop moving toward their destination.

"No!" she blurted with a little too much power. "No, it's fine. I was just wondering if I saved my presentation before I left."

"Oh, that's ok. It'll autosave for you."

"Ahh, yes, right," realizing that her save actually made her seem like a moron. "So, what was it that you were saying?" She forced herself to pay attention to what he was talking about, which was genuinely interesting. Jake had taken the tour of the brewery and was telling her about it, asking her questions every now and then. Had she been to a brewery before, was she new to the area, did she know about all of the new ones popping up, had she heard of the beer diet before because he was thinking of giving it a try.

Conversation with Jake was much easier than it should have been. No one who is this good looking should have to have put so much effort into learning how to talk with people. Ella highly doubted most people who met him had much interest in what he had to say anyway, but maybe that's why he'd gone and made himself very interesting.

When they got to the brewery, it became very obvious that Ella had no idea what kind of beer she liked. In fact, she didn't even like beer very much at all, so she played it off and let Jake order for her, but once again she did a terrible job of playing it off.

"You don't like beer, do you?"

"No, but it's fine! I just haven't had the opportunity to try many kinds, so I'm not really sure what I like," she said, but he stared at her skeptically, ordered the beers and carried them to an open place at a table.

"Cheers, to new friends," he said, raising his cup and clinking it with hers. They were plastic glasses which they were both a little visibly bummed to find out when the "clink" came out as more of a "clonk," and then laughed about their mutual disappointment.

"I hope you don't mind me saying so, Ella, but it doesn't seem like you're very vocal about what you want," Jake said, seemingly out of nowhere.

"Oh, I um—"

"Sorry, I don't mean for that to be critical, though now that I've heard myself say it, I don't see how else it could have been taken. I just mean that, well, in the 15 minutes we've been together so far, you've just gone with the flow even though you were likely busy at work and clearly would have rather gone to a traditional bar."

"Wow, I'm that transparent, huh?" she smiled, knowing that now she had the upper hand with this painfully good-looking person, which she hadn't expected to happen so soon if ever.

"No, I'm not saying that at all. What I'm saying is—"

Ella cut him off and raised her glass. He followed her lead, and she said, "To new beginnings and fresh starts." He smiled, tapped her glass and took a swig. "So, what do you normally do when you're not getting creative with dildos or drinking at breweries?" she asked.

They both laughed, and conversation flowed for the rest of their time together. In fact, it was Ella's calendar notification that alerted her she was about to be late for another event: book club. She explained the situation to him as she reached into her purse to pull out some cash, but he waved her off. "You can get it next time," Jake said. He had one of those flirty smiles that felt like he was winking at you but there was no wink at all. In fact, a wink would have killed the vibe his pearly whites created.

"Want me to walk you back?"

"That would be really nice," Ella responded, a little surprised that she'd taken his advice and asked for what she wanted.

"Look at you, speaking your mind," he said, which made her blush a little.

"So, what's this book club about?" he asked as they walked out of the brewery. "Is it a real book club, or one of those excuses to get together and drink?"

"A little of both," Ella explained. "My friend Mindy and I started it in college with a few friends and we just kept it up after that. We pick a book every month using a poll, so that no one person has to doom us to a terrible book every few months."

Jake genuinely laughed at that. "Right, like *Helvetica* or something."

"To be honest, I'm more worried about the cheap romance novels. They're fine and all, but I just always feel like my time could be better spent reading almost anything else."

"So, what's the book this month?"

"Ironically enough, it is a book about grammar."

"Oh geez."

"But it's actually pretty good! It's called *Wordslut* and it's about how we have gendered our language over time. The content is pretty graphic though, so tonight should be a pretty fun chat."

"Sounds interesting. So, what part of town do you have to get to?"

"My friend Mindy's apartment downtown. Not too far from here. Zora's actually going too, so if she's still at work I'll see if she wants to carpool."

"Oh no, so you're going to tell her everything about this date, aren't you?"

Ella was a little surprised to see this flicker of insecurity coming from him. It was only slight, but enough to endear him to her a little more. "I might," she coyly smiled. "But I didn't know it was a date, I only thought it was a few beers," she flirted.

"It can be a date if you want it to be," he said. "But only if that's what *you* want."

Ella waited a moment. "Then it's a date," she said with confidence and smiled.

14

At some point during the drive to Mindy's apartment, Ella realized that she was barely paying attention to the road at all. She had to ask herself how she'd even gotten this far along, and snapping back to reality.

She still couldn't believe how well the date with Jake had gone, or even that someone as hot as him had wanted to go out with her. As she drove along, Ella wrestled with whether or not she should tell Zora tonight about the date or if she would tell her tomorrow. It was crazy to think that she wouldn't tell her at all though she kind of felt like talking about it would jinx it. But Ella also worried that Jake might tell Zora before she got the chance. How good of friends were they, she wondered to herself.

Ella pulled up to Mindy's high-rise apartment and pulled into the visitor parking in the garage. Of course, Mindy lived in the penthouse, which meant that she had access to more reserve spots than other people in the building. Sometimes they rented the spots out to other residents when they had guests staying over, which wasn't technically allowed, but no one was going to tell Mindy she couldn't do something. Living in the penthouse had its privileges.

All of the other guest parking spots were full which meant that the rest of the group was already there, and Ella was the last to arrive. She grabbed her purse, locked the car, and waved to the doorman on the way in before realizing she'd forgotten her copy of the book in the car.

Ella ran back to her car, yelling at the doorman, "Forgot something in the car, I'll be right back!" She unlocked the car and opened the driver door but didn't see the book. It must have slid under the passenger seat, she thought, and walked over, bending deep into the car until the bright yellow cover finally caught her eye. She stood up, smoothed her outfit again, and hit the lock button on her keys.

As she did, Ella saw someone ducking behind a cement column out of the corner of her eye. Was that... Chad? It couldn't have been. There was no reason he'd be on this side of town let alone this building. She crept around a corner of the parking garage, trying to look nonchalant, but saw no one. Deciding that it was just her brain playing tricks on her, Ella forced a smile, and rushed back to the elevator, remembering that she was holding up the group discussion.

The doorman nodded to Ella. "Visiting Mindy?" he asked.

"Yes, thank you." Ella always felt bad that she didn't know his name but too much time had passed for her to ask now so she just acted as friendly as possible while he swiped a keycard and pressed the PH button. The doors closed and almost instantly Ella felt her ears pop as it shot upwards. She was always impressed by how fast this elevator moved, and before she had a chance to start thinking about whether or not she'd really seen Chad in the garage, the doors opened up and all of the girls sat looking at her from the living room. They threw their arms up and yelled when they saw her.

"She's here!" Mindy yelled the loudest, popping off the couch like there was a spring underneath her, running over to hug Ella. Mindy's hugs always made Ella laugh. They were so firm and heartfelt but somehow light, as though using any kind of force would make them both poof into dust. Of course, Lulu was trailing Mindy with an equally light hug.

"Nice of you to join us," Zora said from the couch, raising her glass of whiskey in Ella's direction, and Ella felt a twinge of guilt that she hadn't already told Zora about her date with Jake. This was her best friend, after all. What was wrong with her?

Trix was off in the corner dancing to the chillhop that was playing, living in her own little world as usual. It never failed to make Ella smile when she saw how authentic Trix was to herself. She always knew exactly what it was she wanted to do, and then she did it.

Before Ella even had a chance to sit down, Mindy had put a mixed drink in an ice hi-ball glass in her hand. They always had a themed drink to start this night and this week was some dual-color concoction that looked like it was sweet enough to induce a diabetic shock.

"So, what are we sipping on tonight?" Ella asked as she took a drink through a paper straw. It tasted exactly like she thought it would.

"Oh, I don't know. It's something Lulu made up—" Mindy said dismissively before Lulu interrupted her.

"It's a mixture of—"

"You can tell her later, Lu. Right now, I've got some big news for you all, now that you're finally here," Mindy said with a level of seriousness that even made Trix stop twirling in the corner and look over at the rest of the group.

15

Mindy loved attention. She loved it almost as much as she loved herself but learned at a young age that the more she loved herself, the easier it was to get other people to love her too. So, when she had everyone's attention, like she did right now, it was the best feeling in the world.

"First of all, thank you all for coming," Mindy started, as though they were here explicitly to hear her big announcement. They stared, urging her to continue. "As you know, Creel and I have been wanting to move in together.

"Who is Creel?" Trix blurted out, as Mindy tried to hide her annoyance. Lulu jumped in so she could pump herself back up.

"Creel is Mindy's *boyfriend*, Trix. They've been together for *three months*," Lulu said, rolling her eyes.

"Huh. Have we met him?" Trix asked, oblivious to how much her questions were annoying Mindy.

"Yes. You have," Mindy answered measuredly.

"Only about *five times*," Lulu continued to come to her idol's rescue. "There was their coming out as a couple party, the Puppy Bowl party before we all boycotted the Super Bowl, Jenny's birthday, and, well, I'm not sure what the other two times were," Lulu admitted, losing steam with it.

"We boycotted the Super Bowl?" Trix asked, confused by so many pieces of this conversation.

"You know what, none of this is the point," Mindy jumped in. "The point is that I'm moving in with Creel. My parents bought a house in the hills above Sunset and so I'll be living there from now on," she announced but received only a small wave of enthusiasm from the group. "Adios, Downtown," she added, trying to get the desired reaction from the group.

Trix clearly couldn't have been more confused by this conversation and drained the rest of her drink. "What kind of a name is Creel anyway?" she asked as she stood with a wobble to pour herself another one. At this question Zora let out a small yelping laugh, but when she saw how mad Mindy was at the lack of excitement over her move, Zora quickly segued it into, "This is so exciting, Mindy. Congratulations! Have you seen the new house?"

Soothed now that the attention was back on her where it was supposed to be, Mindy said, "No. But I've seen pictures."

"Ahhh," Zora said, taking a gulp of her drink instead of biting her tongue.

"This is really exciting, Mind," Ella said, stifling her own laughter and reaching over to hug her friend. "When is the move?"

"End of this month. Don't worry, I've hired movers—"

"And I'll be helping too!" Lulu interjected.

"Yes. Lulu will help too. Thank you, Lu," Mindy patted her friend lightly on the shoulder. "And after I'm moved in, I'll of course have a housewarming party. Anyways, it's going to affect where we have book club from now on, so I just wanted to let you know that this is our last book club in this apartment. Let's savor the moment!" she trumpeted, raising her glass to her friends. They followed her lead and clinked glasses with theirs, except for Trix who was still making her winding way back from the kitchen.

"I still don't know what kind of a name Creel is," she mumbled. Anger quickly flashed over Mindy's face as she realized Trix wasn't going to let this go. "He made it up, ok? Because it's *cool* and *real*. Now can we get on to talking about the book?" she rushed.

"Oh. My. God." Trix said flatly. "Yes, please, let's do anything other than talk about that."

Ella and Zora exchanged a silent laugh and pulled out their copies of the book.

Book club had a strict no phone rule so that they could all be in the moment. So, when they reached for their books, they also did one last glance at their phones before tucking them away. Ella saw that she had an email from one of the jobs she'd applied for across town. Unable to resist, she tapped and opened it.

"Hi Ella,

Thanks for reaching out. We'd love to set up an introductory phone interview with you before bringing you into the office. Are you free tomorrow at 9am? If not, please propose an alternate time in your reply.

Best wishes,

Timothy"

9am was exactly when Ella was supposed to start work, and her boss would finally be in the office tomorrow. She thought about what other time she could propose for a little too long while staring at her screen, prompting Zora to nudge her, "What's that about?"

"Oh! Nothing!" Ella exclaimed a little too quickly, locking her screen and throwing her phone in her bag so hard that it clanked off of something else that was in there. She hoped it was ok, as Zora stared at her for a few more seconds with concern.

Ella was now keeping two things from her best friend. Her date with Jake and potentially leaving the job Zora had stuck her neck out to get her. And then the memory of what she thought was the fleeting glimpse of Chad in the parking lot.

16

Book club had been a little more boozy than usual as they
all attempted to make it "one to remember" while they tried
to come up with fun, non-gendered insults like their book
Wordslut had encouraged them to do. That meant that Ella
was a little later getting into work than she'd planned and
would struggle to reasonably sneak out for her phone
interview at 9am.

Ella had barely even found enough time to look up the
company she was interviewing with, which she always tried
to do before interviews. The one time she hadn't bothered
to do that was for this job and so far, that choice had turned
out to be interesting to say the least.

She turned the corner to get to her desk and saw the back of
a woman's head peeking up from the ergonomic chair in the
workstation next to Ella's own. She took a deep breath and
composed herself, assuming she knew exactly who this
woman was: her new boss.

"Hi," Ella said as she sat her oversized purse on her desk
and turned toward the woman.

"Oh, hi there," the woman said. Now that Ella could see her face, she was a little surprised. This woman was likely in 50s and had a very bookish vibe about her. Ella though she'd look more at home in a library or a trendy bookstore than at a sex toy company, but then again, Ella was pretty sure some people would think she looked out of place too.

"I'm Janet. You must be Ella," this woman with an impeccable topknot said, extending her hand.

"Yeah, Ella. Nice to meet you Janet," Ella tried to sound as enthusiastic as possible.

"It looks like you've settled in nicely," Janet said, and Ella wasn't sure if she was reading too much into her tone by detecting a near-audible eyeroll. Like Ella had gotten too comfortable too quickly, but she told herself that was just her Imposter Syndrome setting in.

"Yup. This is where they told me to sit, so that's what I did," Ella felt awkward, unsure how to respond to something like what Janet had just said.

"Great, well I've worked my way through about 100 emails this morning but have at least 200 more. I'm going to be focused on that until lunch. Want to grab a bite then and talk about what you've been up to while I was out?"

Ella was so thankful for the reprieve, and for the fact that she wouldn't have to think up a weird excuse to do her phone interview. "Sounds great!" she said a little too enthusiastically.

Janet nodded and put on some headphones. Ella sat in her adjacent workstation and booted up her computer. She only had about 10 minutes before her interview and wanted some time to mentally prepare. She took her laptop to make it look like she was going to work elsewhere in the building and went to scope out a quiet call room where she could chat freely.

The recruiter rang her phone right at 9am, which Ella thought was a good sign. The entire conversation lasted about five minutes. It was a pretty standard call. They asked Ella what she wanted —security, benefits, growth potential, parking — and they told her what they could offer — lots of growth potential, benefits, bonuses, parking, and catered lunches. While they didn't highlight the long-term security of the job, Ella knew that was most likely because it's a liability to nearly guarantee security anywhere. She was nearly sold, and they said they'd be in touch about next steps. The only reason she wasn't sold was her fear of letting down Zora.

As Ella was walking back to her desk, her phone buzzed in her hand. She looked at the text:

JAKE: You busy tomorrow night?

"Someone tell you a joke?" a familiar voice asked Ella, who had apparently been smiling as she responded, causing her to snap back to reality. It was Zora, standing in front of Ella. She'd clearly just arrived because she was still holding all of her stuff.

"Z!" Ella said, shocked and relieved. It was time to fill her in. "Come here," she grabbed her friend's arm and guided her to the kitchen.

"Slow down, kid. What's up?"

"So, I went out with Jake last night."

"You sly dog. And you didn't tell me?! How did it go?" Zora asked, forgetting that she had anywhere else to be, like actually working.

"I didn't want to steal Mindy's thunder. It went really great! And he just asked if I wanted to go out tomorrow."

"What did you say?"

"Nothing yet. I just started replying when I saw you. Oh god!" Ella exclaimed, reaching for her phone. "He probably thinks I'm typing a novel from how long it's taken me to respond."

ELLA: I'm free :)

The typing bubble with the ellipsis popped up immediately.

"That was close," Ella said.

"The beginnings of relationships are too volatile," Zora opined. "People are so sensitive and read into the smallest of things. He needs to understand that sometimes people see their friends in hallways and get sidetracked," she smiled at Ella who was staring at her phone.

JAKE: Great! I thought you were turning me down for a second there when I saw you typing.

"See what I mean?" Zora said. "Ok I gotta get going. Chat later?"

Ella nodded, not taking her eyes off her phone and gave Zora a small wave goodbye.

ELLA: Nope! Just saw Zora coming in and got sidetracked. Looking forward to hanging out again. Bummer that Saturday is so far away though. ;)

She assumed this was flirty enough to keep things going for the time being. Besides, she had to get back to her desk before her boss thought that she'd been gone for too long. She locked her phone screen and walked back to her desk, planning to slide into her chair without being noticed, but Janet wasn't at her desk either. Ella breathed a sigh of relief and finally got started on her work for the day.

17

Ella hadn't been on a cute date like this in ages. It was usually just some guy who she met on a dating app or someone who she could only conjure up feelings of friendship no matter how hard she tried. But with Jake everything felt different. She arrived a few minutes late, but instead of waiting in his car, uncomfortable being alone in a place, he'd gone in and got them a booth in the back.

JAKE: Walk in and straight back. See you soon.

The place was a dimly lit bar with Día de Los Muertos sugar skulls decorating the walls. Ella was taken in by the sight of not only the decor and a giant crystalline ceiling-to-floor bar, which was clearly the centerpiece, but also the smells coming from the kitchen and the sounds of laughter seemingly coming from every table. Tequila will do that, she thought. Then she finally saw Jake at the back of the restaurant and gave a little wave.

Even though he was in the back of the booth, Jake stood as much as he was able with the bench seats, gave her a kiss on the cheek and waited until Ella was settled to sit down.

"You made it!" he said, and Ella was a little surprised to see how excited he was to see her.

Much like last time, their conversation was easy, and Ella never found herself looking for the next thing they'd talk about. There were no awkward silences, and the server Jules even had to come back several times to see if they were ready to order yet. By the third time, Jules seemed a little annoyed — and possibly envious, Ella thought? — at the two of them who couldn't stop laughing long enough to order even an appetizer. In the end, they decided to just get a plate of nachos and another drink, both Ella and Jake saying they weren't really that hungry after all.

The truth was that in the back of Ella's mind, she was worried about what was going to happen after dinner. If they ended up bar hopping or back at one of each other's apartments, she didn't want a cheesy chile relleno swimming around in her guts, trying to escape.

So, they stuck with nachos but had a few more tequila sodas before they started thinking about leaving. Ella knew they could have kept talking until they closed down the place, things were going *that* well. But she also knew she had to be sensible. Not only was Jake basically a perfect person, but she also worked with him, so they had to think twice about every next step.

"I'm going to the restroom. Be back in a sec," Ella said, excusing herself before the thought spiral, she was caught in threatened to ruin their night. She didn't want Jake to think for a second that she was losing interest and knew that if she let herself get caught up in her thoughts, she'd lose track of the conversation and pause. So, she got up and went to the restroom.

As she stared at her slightly red face, Ella wished she was one of those people in the movies who could casually splash their face with cold water and quickly snap back to reality. But she knew that if she even attempted that, her mascara would run, her carefully applied contour risked fading, and the baby hairs framing her face would inevitably get damp, making her look like a sweaty mess instead of the refreshed main character she wanted to be.

Instead, Ella just quickly peed and gave herself a stern pep talk while she washed her hands. She looked around to see if anyone was there before she said out loud, "You are valuable, and Jake is definitely in your league. Everyone else is just jealous. You are strong, smart, beautiful, and fun. Everything is fine."

"You tell them, honey!" Ella heard a thin, raspy voice from somewhere in a dark corner that she hadn't noticed before. She squinted to see who the voice came from, but it wasn't until a waif-thin figure creaked out from the shadowy corner that she saw the woman standing there. She was an older woman, holding out a hand towel to her. Ella was clearly startled, all of her summoned confidence gone, and the woman laughed. "Sorry hon, I didn't mean to scare you. I was just coming back from my break and heard your little speech. Hot towel?" she said, extending the towel to Ella.

"Your break? But you were in that corner?"

"Well sometimes I don't like to go through the hassle of walking through the restaurant, so I just move my stool into this dark corner here for a few minutes and no one is the wiser," the bathroom attendant said. Now that she was clearly in the dim light, Ella could see that she had to be in her 70s and that just walking over to Ella had taken a lot of energy. But Ella was shaken up by this encounter, and as much as she wanted to know more about this odd woman, she wanted even more to get out of there.

"Take care," Ella said, not even bothering to find money to tip the woman.

"Thanks hon, and good luck," the woman said, and Ella swore she heard a little cackle under the woman's breath but was equal parts sure that she was just creeped out and probably imagining it.

Once in the hallway with the bathroom door shut, Ella leaned against a wall for a few seconds gathering herself, so she didn't come back to the table looking like she'd seen a ghost. She'd tell Jake this story sometime, but wanted to keep up the vibe, and she'd already been gone from the table for too long.

As her adrenaline settled and Ella became aware of just how buzzed she was from the tequila, she resolved to get back to the table without stumbling and continue having a great night. She took a couple of confident steps down the hallway when she felt a hand clamp down a little too hard on her right shoulder. She hesitantly turned to look behind her, wondering if that woman had followed her out of the bathroom. Then she heard the familiar voice.

"Ella? Is that you?"

18

For a split second, Ella could not find her breath, her footing, or her voice as she stood there staring up at Chad. He was smiling down at her, his hand still on her shoulder. There was something not right with his smile, Ella thought to herself. Was it something sinister? Or was she just imagining it?

"Ella," he said coolly, as though they were long lost family members, not ex-lovers whose restraining order happened to have expired. He pulled her into a hug, wrapping his arms all of the way around her, holding her just tight enough to let her know she couldn't get away if she wanted to. She stood there stiff as a board, not returning the embrace, still trying to figure out if this was a nightmare.

Chad released her from the hug, pushing Ella back but still holding her firmly by both shoulders. "C'mon Ella, don't be like that," he said kindly but with a hint of accusation in his voice. "After all of this time you're not excited to see me?" He laughed a little at what Ella could only imagine was the look of horror on her face.

"Let's try this again," he pulled Ella back into a tighter, constricting hug.

This can't be happening, Ella thought to herself as she stood there in a restaurant bathroom hallway. Her abusive ex had tracked her down and she was trapped. Just then she heard another voice and a new kind of panic set in.

"Ella?" she heard Jake say with an air of confusion.

Chad was reluctant to let Ella go but she fought her way out of his embrace and moved as fast as she could to Jake's side. Chad caught her hand at the last second though and held it for a moment until Ella was able to snatch it back.

"What's going on here?" Jake said, trying to laugh off this awkward encounter. "Are you ok?" he asked Ella. Of course, Jake would be more concerned with me than with why I'm hugging some guy in a dark hallway, Ella thought, while mentally awarding him more points for the move.

"Yes, I'm fine. Can we go?" she started to say, but Chad cut in.

"Oh hi! You must be the boyfriend. I'm Chad," he said enthusiastically to Jake, extending his hand. Jake shook it.

"I'm not sure how that's your business," he said kindly, but noticing Ella's body language also knew he shouldn't be too friendly with this stranger.

"Woah, sorry buddy, didn't mean to push any buttons. I just figured you were together since Ella likes to settle down fast," Chad laughed at his lie, but he was the only one. "I didn't get your name," Chad said to Jake, staring at him eagerly.

"I didn't tell you. Hey, have a good night, Chad, we're going to get out of here," Jake said, ushering Ella away from him.

"It was good to see you El! Hope I run into you again," Chad shouted after them.

Ella didn't dare look back, afraid it would give Chad some sort of validation that his obvious ambush had in some way worked, but she already knew he'd seen the fear in her eyes.

"Hey, let's get out of here and get some fresh air, yeah?" Jake said.

"But the bill?" Ella said, coming around to her senses.

"Already paid."

"I'll Venmo you." Ella had never been so grateful in her life. The moment they got out of the front door she drank in the fresh air, not realizing that she'd been holding her breath for nearly that entire exchange.

How had Chad known she was there? And was he really following her again? She'd thought she'd seen him lurking in the corner of her vision so often lately, so why had he chosen tonight to confront her. There was always the chance it was a coincidence, but Ella found that hard to believe.

The sound of Jake's voice cut through her thoughts, "So who was that guy anyway?" he asked, leading Ella to a quiet bench in the urban park outside of the restaurant.

Ella took a deep breath before saying, "*That* was my ex."

19

Jake offered to take Ella home because she seemed so shaken, but she insisted that she was fine now that they were away from Chad.

"At the very least let me wait for your rideshare with you," Jake said, so Ella let him. She was actually really glad that she'd decided to let him wait on the street with her because truth be told she was still disturbed from the entire encounter. She bristled at every little shadow on the street, wondering if it was Chad just waiting for her to be alone again.

They chatted a little while they waited. It was clear that Jake wanted to know more about that interaction, but that Ella was reluctant to explain anything from a time in her life she'd like to forget. In the moment, it had seemed like getting a restraining order against Chad was the best thing to do, but in retrospect she realized that it had very little effect since she was still scared of running into him. And whenever she told someone who she was dating that she'd done that, they immediately started thinking that she was crazy.

So, when Jake started asking questions, Ella tried to be as vague as possible without seeming evasive.

"How long were you two together?" A normal question from perfectly normal Jake, Ella thought.

"Well, on and off for a couple of years while I found my footing in LA," Ella said.

"A couple of years, wow. And he just... went nuts one day or what?"

"There were some warning signs I should have noticed earlier," Ella said, hoping that he'd drop it there. But she knew that he wouldn't.

"Like what?" Jake said in a genuinely curious tone that made Ella want to continue opening up to him. Her car was now in sight, so she knew there wasn't enough time to get to the bad details anyway.

"Well, he was really possessive. He never liked when I went out with my friends. A few times I caught him following me when we went to a bar or something. That was one of the times we broke up," she paused, waiting to see his reaction.

96

"Yeah, that does sound a bit nuts. Stuff like tonight wasn't unusual for you then?"

"Well, it is now because I haven't seen him in a few years. I thought I was finally rid of him," she gave him her most honest answer. Now that the adrenaline rush of seeing Chad was subsiding, Ella was becoming aware of just how much she'd had to drink. She could feel a case of the spins creeping up on her and knew the only way to keep it at bay was to stare at something in the distance. Unfortunately, this made her look more pensive and affected than she really was. At this point she just didn't want to throw up before she made it home.

Jake snapped her back to the moment saying, "Is that your car?" A black sedan was waiting on the street, and since they were the only ones around Ella assumed it was hers, but double checked the app anyway to confirm.

"Yeah, yeah it is. Sorry for zoning out there for a minute," Ella said, gathering herself. "Thanks again for everything. I wish it had ended a bit better," she said looking to Jake.

"It's totally fine!" Jake said, a little too enthusiastically. "Life happens, I get it," he toned it down.

"Ok well, I guess I'll call you," Ella said hesitantly, reacquainting herself with the situation she was currently in. Second date meant they usually kissed, but was this really a date? And was that appropriate under the circumstances? Jake seemed to be having the same dilemma and they both leaned in for a hug. A hug that friends might give each other after not seeing one another for a while. Then Jake walked over, opened her door, and helped Ella in."

"Mind letting me know when you get home safe?" he asked with a sheepish smile. "I promise it doesn't count as your 'I'll call you.' I just want to make sure you're ok, you know. Especially given the circumstances."

That was about the sweetest thing Ella could remember a man saying to her and for a moment she forgot all about Chad, and the spins, and everything else that was going on. It was just sweet, smiling Jake.

"Sure thing," she said, and he closed the door.

"You two make a pretty cute couple," the driver said, looking back at her. Ella honestly hadn't even registered his presence outside of a driving capacity until this moment.

The driver was an older man who the app said was named Mel. He smiled at her, waiting for a reply but Ella could come up with nothing other than, "Oh! Thank you."

Mel seemed to understand something unspoken between them that she was in no shape to chat and mercifully let them ride the rest of the way in silence.

The ride was short, or at least it seemed that way to Ella's buzzed brain that was replaying the good, the bad, and the ugly of the night in her mind. She realized she hadn't even checked her phone all night, and as she saw all of the notifications she'd missed and a panic attack started washing over her, it was cut short by Mel's voice.

"We're here," he said cheerfully.

"Oh, oh wow that was fast. Thank you," she said getting out of the car and seeing a new notification pop up to rate her ride and tip him. 5 stars and $5 she thought to herself, trying to be mindful about the action so that she'd remember she'd tipped him when the question of 'what if' bombarded her when she was trying to sleep, causing her to check her phone or otherwise nag at her all night.

Ella mindlessly walked up her stairs, unlocked her door and plopped down on her couch to rest for a few minutes, when a text from Jake popped up on her screen.

JAKE: You get home ok?

Yes, God, just give me a minute please, Ella thought to herself then immediately followed it up with a self-chastisement. "He's just being a good person, you asshole," she said aloud in the empty apartment.

Then with every ounce of energy left in her, Ella pushed herself up off the couch, walked to the kitchen and poured the rest of an open bottle of wine into a large glass, then plopped back down on the couch.

Ella unlocked her phone, opened their texts, and typed back:

ELLA: Yup! Just got settled in. Thanks again for being great.

She sent it, quickly scrolled through the rest of the notifications she'd received — none were important — and stared at the glass of wine for a few moments before chugging it and falling asleep.

20

The next morning, Ella woke up with a dull headache — not the splitting kind after a long night out but the kind that throb all day, never letting up. Too strong for ibuprofen but too mild to warrant the prescription of anything stronger.

Ella had eventually fallen asleep, though she wasn't sure at what time. It was apparent that she had managed to put herself in bed and use one of the emergency face cleansing wipes that she kept next to her bed for cases just like tonight. So, when the alarm went off —which she didn't remember setting either — she just laid there staring at the ceiling, debating whether or not to call out sick.

After the snooze went off two more times and she hadn't been able to stop the steady river of thoughts running through her mind nor had she been able to motivate herself to get out of bed, Ella unlocked her phone to type an email to her manager Janet.

Hey Janet,

I hate to do this, but I think I ate some bad food last night and have food poisoning. I'm going to take a sick day to recover and will be back in tomorrow.

Best,
Ella

Ella never knew what the appropriate salutation in an email was. She deeply admired the people who were able to confidently sign off with a simple *Cheers* in any situation. Or those unicorns who could get away with a *Sincerely* without sounding like jerks.

After Ella hit send on the email, she knew she had to text Zora next so that she wouldn't worry when Ella wasn't there. But then Ella started wondering if Zora would even notice her best friend wasn't there.

"I'm not even going down that rabbit hole," Ella said aloud to herself.

ELLA: Hey! I just wanted to let you know I'm not coming in today and didn't want you to worry.
ZORA: Oh? Everything ok?

ELLA: Yeah, I just need a day to chill. But if Janet asks, I had food poisoning. Poke is my number one suspect. *wink*

ZORA: Yikes. Ok take care of yourself girl. Let me know if you need anything. Take naps.

Ella wanted to tell Zora about seeing Chad but then she'd have to go into the rest of what happened on the date too, and she wasn't sure why, but Ella wasn't really into talking about encountering Chad.

She went back to sleep and had one of those great morning dreams that feel so much more vivid than a night dream. In this particular one, Ella was on top of the world. She was the queen of the 4th of July parade in the small town she grew up in. Her friends were sitting behind her on the float, and Jake was there as Prince Charming. Nothing notable happened in the dream; Ella just kind of woke up.

Realizing it was 10am, Ella made herself get out of bed and get some water. She knew she'd have a ton of notifications on her phone, not because she was popular but because she enabled too many of them. So, she decided to tackle that right now.

It took an entire episode of some ghost hunter show that was playing in the background, but Ella felt good about how many fewer times her phone would chirp at her now. But before she could finish the thought, a text popped up from Zora.

ZORA: You went out with Jake again and didn't tell me?? I'm starting to wonder if we're even friends...

Ella knew there was a chance Jake had told her and that this was coming.

ELLA: That's because I'm trying to forget about it. The date was fine but we ran into Chad...
ZORA: OMG! Now I'm even more upset that you didn't tell me about this. That explains why Jake didn't want to go in detail when he mentioned it.
ELLA: What did he say?

She was suddenly curious about how Jake was characterizing the night to other people.

ZORA: Nothing really. He just asked me if I knew how you were doing. I guess he thought we were friends or something and that we told each other stuff...

Ella could nearly hear Zora's only half joking sarcasm through the text.

ELLA: I know, I know, I'm sorry.

ZORA: So, what happened???

ELLA: One minute I was going to the bathroom, the next I was walking back to the table and Chad was just standing there. And he hugged me like we're best friends. Then Jake walked up and saw us and I'm sure it looked terrible.

ZORA: That sounds rough. So how did it end?

ELLA: Jake waited with me for a car and I went home.

ZORA: No! The part with Chad. He just went away quietly?

ELLA: Yeah I think so. Tbh I was pretty shocked so I don't remember everything exactly.

ZORA: Girl, that's awful. No wonder you took the day off. Janet came up here asking to see if you were ok too.

That genuinely shocked Ella. She wasn't even aware that Janet knew she and Zora were best friends.

ELLA: She did? That's weird.

ZORA: Yeah, well new ppl normally don't call in sick after this short of a time on the job. I told her you were going to be ok though. Bad poke.

Ella was pretty sure there was some judgement coming her way from Zora but she also reminded herself not to read too much into a text.

ZORA: I've got to get back to work, but can we catch up tonight? Please!
ELLA: Yup. The usual?
ZORA: See you there.

Ella locked her phone and was pleased that a whole hour went by before she received any more notifications.

21

As the time got closer when Ella and Zora were supposed to meet, Ella kept hoping more and more that her friend would cancel on her and she could stay home. But that didn't happen, so when Ella got a text from Zora that she was leaving work, Ella rushed to get ready and head down the street to their usual bar.

She got there before Zora did, and instead of grabbing a moody booth in the back like she usually would, for some reason today Ella felt like sitting at the bar top. This room was darkly lit and always a bit smokey. It made her feel like she could disappear even in the middle of the room. In fact, she almost succeeded when Zora walked past her heading back toward their booth, but Ella gently grabbed her friend's shoulder as she passed.

Zora looked up, genuinely surprised.

"What are you doing over here?" she asked.

"I don't know, it just felt right to sit over here today."

"Well, you take one day off and you're all of a sudden a new person," Zora joked as she searched under the bar top for a hook to hang her purse, but found none, placing it on her lap instead.

The bartender walked by, and Ella waved him down, and pointing to her martini said, "One more please."

"Since when do you order for me?" Zora asked her.

"Oh, no that was for me," Ella said, gulping down the drink that was in her hand as Zora stared wide eyed at her.

"I'll have what she's having," Zora said to the bartender, then turned back to Ella. "Ok, what's going on with you. You're being really secretive lately. Are you depressed?" the voice was concerned.

Zora was known for getting to the point, but Ella wasn't used to her saying things she hadn't yet thought about herself. Was she depressed? "I don't think so," Ella started. "There's just been a lot going on lately, and I realize this is going to sound crazy—"

Ella was cut off by the bartender handing them drinks.

"Thanks, hey, could you actually just pour a shot of whiskey. I need a little liquid courage," Ella said, waiting for the shot before continuing.

"Sheesh, you really are going through it," Zora said, sipping from her own drink.

The bartender handed Ella the shot and she threw it back then handed him the empty shot glass.

"I think Chad is following me again," Ella blurted out before she could rethink putting those words into the ether.

"You what??" Zora said in surprise, nearly doing a spit take.

"Zora, I know this sounds crazy, but I seriously think he's following me again. I thought I saw him the other day in Mindy's garage, and then last night at the restaurant. I don't know if I manifested him there because I'd been thinking about whether or not I'd seen him, but it really freaked me out."

Zora just quietly sipped from her drink, letting Ella get everything out and waiting until she was sure Ella was finished, which she wasn't quite yet.

"And then when they were doing the background check for this job, I wondered if it would show up that I'd had a restraining order against him and if they'd think I was crazy for that and — *was* I crazy for that? Was he really stalking me or was I just annoyed? And then there is Jake who is so perfect, and I just know I'm going to screw this up because I'm screwed up and who wants to date someone with this much baggage? And that's why I haven't been telling you about my dates with him because I don't want to jinx it. How's all of that for starters?" Ella said, looking spent and immediately finishing half of her fresh martini in one gulp.

"Well, that's a lot," Zora coolly said with a smile. "First of all, don't worry about the Jake stuff. You don't have to tell me about the dates just because he does. And he's really into you, by the way. He felt bad you had to deal with that drama last night, but I don't think he seemed put off by it." Ella visibly exhaled when Zora said this.

"And as for the Chad stuff, well, you said it was traumatic and that's going to stick with you. But you have to keep in mind that this is a small city and you both live in it, so there's a good chance you'll continue running into each other. That's why you liked him so much to begin with. You had almost all of the same likes and dislikes, remember?"

Ella nodded her head.

"If I'm being honest — you're going to want to finish your drink for this one," Zora said, nodding to the rest of Ella's martini. "I don't think Chad has any problems that a little therapy couldn't fix. Besides the weird jealousy issues, he was a normal dude."

Ella was flabbergasted. "Weird jealousy issues?!" Ella asked using air quotes to emphasize how idiotic she thought that was. "Zora, he followed me around for months!"

"Listen, I knew you weren't going to like hearing that, but I mean it. I think he was just really infatuated with you, combined with a lot of jealousy. I'm not devaluing your feelings. You are entitled to feel however you want, I just want you to try and step back now that time has gone by and think of them objectively. Maybe that's why your brain is playing these tricks on you."

On one hand, Ella knew that Zora could be right, that she sometimes did get too wrapped up in the stories she told herself, but on the other she couldn't believe what she was hearing. Without much warning, Zora stood up, put her purse over her shoulder, finished her drink and hugged Ella.

"I've got a sound bath class to teach down the street, so I've got to go, but don't stay here too much longer, ok? I'll see you tomorrow," Zora said before striding out the door.

Ella watched her go and sat there feeling suddenly alone. Then her gaze was drawn to a familiar face sitting at the corner of the bar staring at her: Chad.

22

In that moment, Ella felt emotions flicker over her face as fight or flight kicked in, her brain unsure of what her body should do. So, she just stared at him wide eyed before awkwardly turning back to the bar and getting another drink.

She kept her back to Chad and considered slinking back into a booth and disappearing, but she didn't want him to find her back there and trap her into conversation. Leaving wasn't an option because she was a little two wobbly on her legs. When the bartender dropped off another martini she asked for water as well this time, and the check.

Ella wasn't positive that Chad was still there, staring at her from the other side, but she thought she could feel his eyes on her, and she was too nervous to look. The only option was to act nonchalant, which would be a difficult task in this state. Her alcohol buzz was going strong, and as she sipped the fresh martini, making sure not to gulp it down, she was sure this one would put her over the drunk edge.

A few minutes went by, and the bartender never brought Ella the check, so she flagged him down.

"Hi, can I get the check please? I asked for it a little while ago."

"Oh, it's been paid for. That guy down there at the end of the bar," the bartender said. Ella froze, trying not to be furious but trying even harder not to look to where she knew Chad was sitting.

"Why would you let him do that?" she growled.

"I'm— um, well I'm sorry about that. No one's ever complained about a tab being picked up for them before," he said, seeming genuinely confused over the whole thing. "Want me to refund him and give you the check?" he asked, turning to Chad, but when both he and Ella looked over, Chad was gone, and all that was left was his empty glass.

Ella sighed. "No, I guess it's ok. Thank you, and I'm sorry. He's my ex," she tried to explain.

Bartender nodded in a knowing way and headed into the back room to get more ice.

It was a relief, Ella thought to herself as she let out a breath she didn't know she'd been holding in, and continued to sip her drink. To her left, she saw a person settle in a few chairs down and smelled cigarettes. She knew who it was before she even looked, but there was nowhere to run now without seeming insane, Bartender wasn't there to help her. Facing him was the only way to deal with this.

Ella turned her head but was careful not to turn her body toward him, indicating she wasn't really interested in talking but wasn't going to run either. He was smiling at her, giving the same warm yet somehow creepy smile he'd given her last night at the restaurant.

"What are the odds of me running into you two days in a row?" Chad said, trying to break the ice, but careful not to inch closer to her, as if he could see the thin bubble of self-control that was surrounding her.

"Probably pretty good since you've been following me," Ella muttered under her breath.

"What's that?" he said, unable to hear her quip.

"The odds are pretty low," she recovered, adding, "Thanks for the drink."

"No problem. So, what are you up to these days?" he tried to start a conversation, careful to not physically cross over the one-seat space that was between them.

"Just living my life, nothing special," Ella curtly said, hoping he'd get the hint and go away. When he took a moment to respond she thought maybe the message was received.

"Look, Ella. I'm sorry, okay? I was really lost when you ended things and I acted like a total nut," he said honestly, which took her aback and without thinking she turned more of her body toward him. "I went to therapy, and I've been really happy since then. I got a promotion at work and I'm managing the East Side office we just opened up over here. In fact, I just moved into that little blue building across the street over there," he said, and Ella went numb. There was only one little blue building across the street, and it was the one she also lived in. She went silent again.

"I understand if you don't want to talk anymore, but I'd really like if we could be friends again or at the very least be civil since we keep running into each other," Chad said in a

116

tone so reasonable that Ella felt like a bitch if she didn't at least consider his request. She thought about what Zora had said earlier about Chad, and Zora was one of the most rational people Ella knew.

Ella turned her body away from Chad and back toward Bartender as she swirled the green olive at the bottom of her nearly empty glass, then set it down and reached for her water.

"Ok, I can take a hint," Chad said, downing his drink, only to turn back toward Ella and see her hand outstretched towards him. He smiled, she returned a half smile, and they shook hands. "We're not friends. I don't want to hang out, but we can be civil," she said, feeling very mature and in control. She couldn't wait to tell Zora about this later.

"That's all I want," Chad said, standing to leave. "See you around, Ella," he said with a nod and walked out.

Ella sipped her water as she waited a few minutes to make sure he was long gone before she too got up and walked out the door.

23

The air was heavier than it had been when she'd entered the bar, Ella was sure of it. Something had shifted and now everything felt dark and ominous. She didn't know why her heart was still racing. Everything had seemed ok with Chad, at least as far as how he seemed now. But she still couldn't shake the feeling of being watched.

"You ok, lady?" the security guard startled her with the question. Where had he come from, she thought to herself. She'd just looked around for Chad, so where had this guy been while she was doing that?

"Uh, yeah, I'm fine," she said, staring back suspiciously as she walked across the street. The closer she walked to her building, the more exposed she was, and without realizing it, she broke out into a trot. Reaching the door to her building, Ella fumbled with her keys, accidentally trying to use the one for her unit door in the front door. Eventually she heard the locks tumble into place, and she dashed upstairs to her apartment.

Living on the third floor meant that she always had the option of stairs or elevator and while being confined in a stairway sent a chill up Ella's spine, the idea of having to wait for an elevator was even more uncomfortable. So, by the time she reached her door she was panting. Getting the correct key into the correct lock this time, Ella slammed the door behind her.

It was so hard to breathe that Ella felt herself gasping from air, not so much from the run up the stairs, but for another reason she didn't understand. There was a tightness in her throat that wasn't letting up even though she was inside now. Her heart was beating faster than she'd ever remembered, and even her eyesight was getting fuzzy.

I've got to sober up, Ella thought to herself, walking over to the fridge and pulling out her filtered water pitcher. It was empty. So, she set it on the counter, then turned on the faucet and gulped down a glass of tap water, not wanting to take the time to have to filter new water. But after gulping down two cups of tap, she said a prayer that there were no weird parasites in there like she'd seen in the news stories, and made the effort to fill up the filtered tank.

Watching the water trickle down into the empty bottom tank of the filter was somewhat calming and mesmerizing. Without realizing it, Ella stood there watching it until the dripping stream of clean water blended into the now full lower tank of the pitcher. Snapped back to the room, Ella poured herself a glass of clean water, refilled the filter tank, put it back in the fridge then went to sit down.

She felt better. As she started replaying the afternoon in her mind, Ella felt an odd idea begin to form. Maybe Chad really was ok now. After all, Zora was the most rational person she knew and even she said that Ella might have been overreacting when they broke up.

Ella took a deep breath and did what she knew was the worst idea ever: took a trip down memory lane. She clicked into the depths of her photos archive and found endless pictures of her and Chad, laughing and happy together. Them together at the aquarium, camping, out to dinner, on a boat. There were also some sweet candids they'd taken of each other around the house, and without realizing it, Ella found herself smiling in real life.

She scrolled a few more times before her phone buzzed. It was a text message from a private number. That set Ella on edge, but curiosity got the better of her and she opened it. There was no text, just a video file. Assuming it was a spam virus Ella was about to delete it when she took a closer look at the preview still frame. It was from inside her old apartment.

Ella took a deep breath, getting up the courage to open the video and tapped it. She was trying to decipher what was going on in the video but still couldn't because everything was so dark. The slivers of blue that moved into the screen as the camera holder moved around was the only light in the frames.

Five seconds into the video Ella still couldn't tell where the video was taken or what was in it, let alone who was taking it. Then a figure finally started to enter the frame. It was a person, she was sure of that, but she still couldn't make out who it was. Finally, the camera stopped moving, fully fixated on the person who it now looked like was laying down. A light flashed across the screen, like something was coming in through a window, and illuminated the person for a brief second.

Ella rewound the video and tapped to pause it on that moment, giving her a better view of who it was. She gasped.

The person was her. She was in her bed sleeping, in the apartment she shared with Chad. And someone, most likely Chad, was standing there watching her sleep and filming her.

A feeling of dread and overall creepiness crawled over Ella as she kept watching. Nothing happened. He stood there filming her sleeping for another two minutes before ending the recording.

She wanted to delete the video and forget she'd ever seen it, but it was too late for that now. After picking up and setting down her phone a few times, Ella decided to watch it again. Usually when she watched a scary movie, it was less scary the second time because she already knew what was going to happen, so she hoped that's what would happen this time.

Ella hit play again and watched it, looking for any sign of something that could confirm her suspicions it was Chad who took the video. While knowing it was him would of course creep her out, she also needed to know that it wasn't someone else who had taken the video. That someone hadn't broken into her apartment and used her phone to take a video of her at her most vulnerable. But even on the second watch, the video gave away nothing. She locked her phone then set it down as she got up to pour herself a glass of wine.

She emptied half a bottle of red wine into a large glass and walked back to her couch, sipping as she had a staring contest with her locked phone.

She tried to be objective about what happened. On one hand, didn't couples think it was cute when the other one watched them sleep? Wasn't this kind of like that? Chad had just thought she was so beautiful when she was sleeping that he wanted to keep the memory. But there was something about him using her phone to do it. Like he wanted her to know he could control every part of her life if he wanted to.

The longer she tried to convince herself it was a cute gesture, the more Ella felt like it was an actual threat. And then there was the whole issue of not being able to confirm it was Chad, but really, who else could it be, she kept telling herself. The video didn't widen enough to show the rest of the bed so she couldn't see if he'd been lying next to her or not.

Ella decided she was done keeping this paranoia to herself and needed someone to talk her down, so she sent the video to Zora.

ELLA: Look what I found on my phone. It's me. Totally freaked out right now. Have no idea who took it, but I think it was Chad.

Zora didn't reply immediately, which Ella kind of thought she wouldn't since she had the sound bath workshop. Now that she'd passed the buck on giving reason to the situation, Ella busied herself doing other things. She tried to read a book, but quickly tired of that, so she decided to make some dinner.

There was next to nothing in her fridge, but at least she could make some eggs. So, she cracked two into the pan, added salt, pepper, and some butter then scrambled them together. It took less than five minutes, which Ella was disappointed in because she was trying to kill time.

She sat down to eat, looking at her phone to see if Zora had texted back. She hadn't but Ella did have a call from a missed number and a voicemail. Probably a scammer, Ella thought to herself, but clicked to listen anyway.

The message was a minute long. A minute of silence, which Ella decided to leave playing while she ate a big bite of the eggs, but at the end of the message she heard breathing and then the click of the caller hanging up.

24

After getting that call, Ella was paralyzed with fear, and she dealt with it the only way she knew how: drinking herself to sleep. When the alarm on her phone buzzed the next morning, Ella thought that maybe she should look into therapy or some other good meds after all. Her head was pounding, and her mouth tasted like a disgusting mix of stale wine and morning breath. That alone was enough to get her out of bed to go brush her teeth and get moving.

One look in the mirror and Ella was mortified. Her eyes were totally swollen from the alcohol, dehydration, and crying. She threw some cold water on her face which didn't help, so she tossed some under eye masks into the freezer to wear while she drove into work.

Checking her phone, she was running about 15 minutes behind and went into her morning routine autopilot. She finished her 9-step skin care routine that she'd seen in a magazine recently, then went out to the kitchen and flicked on the coffee pot while she went back into her room and threw an outfit together. Her head was pounding so it was too hard to come up with anything cute and she went with a black tee and jeans.

Ella slipped on some flats, poured her coffee into a travel mug, and headed out. Right as she was about to lock her door she remembered the eye masks, grabbed them from the freezer and placed them under her eyes. The cool from them instantly felt soothing and it was the first time all morning she'd felt any kind of relief.

Finally, behind the wheel and heading to work, Ella sipped her coffee and her headache began to subside. She'd kill for a breakfast burrito right now but knew that wasn't in the cards since she was already running late. The monotony of her commute also let the events of last night seep back into her mind. The terror she'd felt when she got that call. It had to have been Chad, right?

Whatever it was, it was creepy. Ella considered going to the police with the tape and asking them to help her but what could they do? They had real crimes to worry about, murders and rapes and drug busts and all of that. But maybe they could trace the number for her. When she got to work, Ella decided she'd ask Zora; she'd know what to do. And in the meantime, she just had to try to not panic. Then she remembered Zora hadn't returned her text last night and started worrying about her friend. Was she ok, Ella wondered?

Ella pulled into the parking lot at her work, trying to act like nothing was wrong and maybe trying a little too hard. She waved at the parking attendant who waved back but Ella was sure that she detected a different expression than normal. Was it pity? Ella decided to be even more confident than she thought she was being. As she passed Marley, she said importantly, "Hey Marley! I'm running late but let's get a drink sometime. We've never really had a chance to hang out."

"Yeah! Sounds good!" Marley said excitedly. "But hey, Ella..." Marley tried to continue.

"Can't talk now! Ella said rushing past, confused at what she was doing. Is this what she thought confident people were like — self-important assholes? There was no time to question herself now. She had to get up to Zora right now before this panic attack brewing inside her grew stronger. She set her stuff at her desk. Janet was already in and turned to say hello to Ella but let out a slight gasp.

"Geez, I know I had a rough night, but was it that bad?" Ella joked, now genuinely concerned that she might as well have 'I'm Hungover' tattooed on her forehead.

"No, it's not that. It's just that—" Janet started but Ella cut her off.

"Hold that thought. I've got to run to the restroom. Be right back," Ella said as she ran not to the restroom but right upstairs to Zora's desk. Jake wasn't there, thank God, Ella thought. She planned to refresh her makeup as soon as she explained what happened.

"Zora!" Ella blurted a little too loudly, but she was relieved to see her there. Zora was a little startled then turned around and jumped.

"Oh my God! Ella! What is wrong with you?"

"Sorry, I didn't mean to startle you and I know I look a little rough right now—"

"Yeah, I'll say," Zora reached up towards my eyes and I flinched, trying to swat away her hands.

"What are you doing?!" Then Ella felt Zora's long, delicate fingertips under my eyes pulling off the eye masks.

"Did you forget about these?" Zora asked, laughing.

Ella stood there mortified. So that's why everyone was acting so weird when they saw her. She brushed it off and continued, pulling out her phone and navigating to the video.

25

"What the hell is this?" Zora asked as Ella showed her the video. Apparently, it had been too big to send and the text last night never went through. "Just give me the phone. You're shaking too much," she said, taking the phone away from Ella and holding it closer to her face.

Zora watched the video a few times before she let Ella talk. "I think Chad took this," Ella blurted out, already seeing Zora's eyes start to roll a little. "Let me explain before you tell me I'm paranoid! I saw him at the bar last night, after you left, and —."

"Again?!" Zora said too loudly, drawing a few stares from the people around them. "You saw him again?!" she said, now over correcting and talking barely above a whisper.

"Yes. I waited until after he left before I went home. I didn't want him to see which apartment I went into."

"But isn't your name on the mailboxes?" Zora asked. "It wouldn't be hard to figure out which was yours with a little bit of amateur detective work."

"Shit." Ella hadn't thought of that. One more thing to worry about. "Anyways," she pressed on, "He asked if we could be friends since we kept running into each other. I said sure because I didn't want to seem rude."

"Of course. Women always need to take care of the sensitive male ego," Zora said, now actually rolling her eyes.

"Anyways, he leaves then I leave, then I get this video from a private number, and I'm totally freaked out. Should I go to the police?" Ella asked, desperate for some inkling of a sense of safety.

"You can if you want, but they're pretty useless. With stuff like this they can't do anything until after something happens to you."

"Oh my God, you think something is going to happen to me?!"

"No! No, I don't. Settle down, take a breath. But I've changed my mind and now I do think Chad is a total creep. You need to find a whole new set of places to hang out."

"You're probably right," Ella agreed, a little deflated. Of course Zora was right. It was disappointing that since Chad was following her, *she* had to change *her* life, but that's just how it had to be. "Ok so no police, and find new places to hang out."

"And send me that video. If something *does* happen to you, I'll need to show it to the police," Zora added matter-of-factly.

"So, you DO think something is going to happen to me?!" Ella yelled, making herself the center of the gazes this time.

"No! I don't. But this is really weird, El, and you can't be too safe. Chad is a total weirdo and you need to be smart."

Zora was right; Ella knew it. She handed Zora her phone. "Here, you send it to yourself; I can't handle seeing it again."

Taking the phone from her friend, Zora navigated to Ella's videos when an email message popped up. The subject line read, "Interview details." She swiped away and handed Ella back her phone. "There's an email you got that you might want to read."

"What? Who's it from?" Ella asked, panicking that it was something else from the mystery sender.

"Just see for yourself. I've got to get back to work," Zora said. Ella was a little put off by how terse her friend had suddenly become, but she was sure this wasn't how Zora had planned to spend her morning.

"Thanks, Z," Ella said, taking her phone and tapping open her email as she walked down to her desk. When she saw the one unread item in her inbox, she nearly fell down the stairs and understood why Zora had reacted that way.

26

The more she thought about her name on the mailbox, out there for the world to see, Ella knew she had to move. The chances of Chad going by her exact building and finding her were slim, and besides E. Morris was common enough for him to not be positive that it was her, Ella Morris.

Ella crept into the rabbit hole of seeing how quickly she could find her address listed online — only minutes. Next thing she knew, she was investigating much she could find out about herself online and it was frightening. Within 30 minutes, she'd found pictures she didn't even know were on the internet, bylines she'd forgotten about years ago, and her addresses going back to when she paid her first taxes at 18 years old.

Realizing she still had a ton of work to do, Ella forced herself back up from this black hole and threw herself into every task, trying to distract from the familiar presence of anxiety wrapping its tendrils around her, threatening to make this day one long panic attack.

Then she remembered — the interview! Ella picked up her phone and emailed back quickly to confirm the interview the next day. It was in the afternoon, so she'd have to say she had a doctor's appointment or fake sick, but she told herself it was worth it. She was really starting to like her current job, but as usual she couldn't stop herself from wanting to see what's out there, even if it meant pissing Zora off a little bit.

As soon as Janet had pulled out of the parking lot, Ella rushed to her car and headed home too. She pulled up to her building, giving everything a suspicious once over, then headed up to her apartment. Barely remembering to lock the door, she spotted her computer from across the room, ran over to it and started looking for apartments. She knew she couldn't afford much more than the $1,200 she was paying right now, but even if it was a hole-in-the-wall, it was a way she could get out of here and the internet wouldn't know where she was for at least a little while, which meant Chad wouldn't know where she was.

She sat down and searched for "apartments in Los Angeles." She set the highest price for $1,200 and started looking at one bedrooms. The map was blank. So, she dropped it down to studio apartments, and saw a couple of apartments pop up on the map. The pictures made Ella realize this was not going to work. She considered herself a strong, independent woman who could take on a lot, but these apartments were in neighborhoods that she had no business being in.

She bumped up her search to apartments that were $1,500 a month. A few appeared on the map in safer areas, some that were even close to Ella's job. Once she started reading the details though, she learned that every single one required her to make 2.5x the rent amount every month, and $1,500 was already going to take up a full paycheck and then some. Even without that, she knew she couldn't scrape together the $2,000 it was going to cost for the deposit.

Ella sighed, realizing she was starting to spiral out of control. She had so much debt, didn't make enough money, and couldn't interview at a new place without alienating her best friend and looking flaky at her current job.

The wine bottle in front of her was empty. She could either open a new one or go to bed. Choosing the latter, Ella got up and washed her face. Maybe she couldn't control everything in her life, but she could control whether or not she helped her skin look less puffy in the morning.

Feeling the warm water splash onto her face, Ella started to relax a little. She had to hold her breath when she rinsed off her cleanser which helped her breathing slow a little. I didn't even know I was breathing hard, she thought to herself as she patted her face dry and walked into her bedroom, pulling on the coziest pajama set she owned.

As the minutes ticked by, Ella was feeling more and more relaxed, paying attention to each task she was doing instead of letting her panic run wild. She settled down in bed and had a sense of peace, that maybe everything would end up working out in the end. She wasn't sure how, but now she had faith that it would.

27

After a good night's sleep, Ella woke up feeling like a new person. "This is it," she said out loud to no one. "This is the day I start turning my life around." With her interview today front-of-mind, she grabbed her phone and emailed her manager.

Hi Janet,
I'm feeling under the weather again today and can't come in.
Sorry for the inconvenience.
Best,
Ella

Should she tell Zora too? If she didn't, Zora would text her. If she did, Zora would probably know she was lying because if she was sick enough to miss work, she wouldn't be thinking about who else to tell. Ella decided not to tell Zora, and got on with her morning, praying this didn't make her look terrible for taking two sick days so close together.

In the back of her closet, Ella always kept an interview outfit clean, pressed and ready to go. One time in college she'd gotten a big interview offer with a local magazine, but she was in a lecture hall wearing sweats when she got the email. She ran out of class, across campus, praying that there was something clean in her closet. When she got there, all of her business clothes were clean but so badly wrinkled that it would take at least 15 minutes to press the creases out of them. That's when she learned her lesson to always have one clean, pressed business outfit ready at all times.

Desperate for any outfit, she tugged on a black sweater, some black jeans, and ran out the door again. It wasn't until she was in the sunlight that she realized her hot pink bra was visible through the stitches in her sweater. She sighed and kept walking toward what turned out to be a disastrous interview.

Shaking off those memories, Ella pulled out the clean, pressed interview outfit, hung it on her door jamb, then went off to do her hair and makeup. While looking in the mirror, she made sure to tell herself lots of affirmations.

I am smart.
I am capable.
I am the right person for this job.
I am confident.

I am likable.

She said so many affirmations that by the time she left the bathroom, Ella firmly believed she was ready to take on the world. Grabbing her outfit from the hanger, she pulled on the slacks. They were a perfect fit. Then she put on the top, and that's when she saw it. A big brown blotch staring out from the middle of the white button-up shirt.

"NO!" she yelled in horror, forgetting all of the hype she'd been telling herself. "How could this happen?"

Not waiting for herself to answer, Ella started tearing through her closet. Surely a blazer would cover this up, she thought to herself, but all of her blazers had wrinkles.

"Just take seven minutes to iron the blazer and pay whatever you have to for parking to make it on time," she said aloud. She fumbled around her closet trying to find the iron she rarely used, eventually found it, then plugged it in to heat up while she ran off to her closet to get her least wrinkled blazer.

Ironing took less time than she'd thought it would, but still behind schedule, Ella rushed out of her house, first checking to make sure she had her purse, keys, wallet, and phone. As she turned the key to lock the front door, she remembered: The iron! She hurriedly ran back in and unplugged the iron, which was still sitting hot on top of the ironing board.

28

Ella pulled up to the building and was a little surprised. Since it was in the middle of the city, she'd envisioned a high rise... or at least a three-story building. But instead, this looked like some kind of warehouse near the Metro, LA's subway system. There was plenty of parking, which was a rarity, but also gave Ella a sense of unease. What *was* this place?

Pulling into a spot not too near the front door but not in the back of the lot either, Ella looked at her watch and realized she was miraculously five minutes early. She flipped down the mirror in her driver's seat visor and smiled to make sure there was no lipstick on her teeth. She'd hurriedly done her makeup on the drive over, not realizing she'd have the luxury of five whole minutes before she went in.

Satisfied that every hair was in place, Ella grabbed her purse and reached for the folder of printed resumes that she kept in her car at all times. She opened the cover only to find it empty.

This better not be a sign for how this interview is going to go, Ella thought to herself as she threw her head back against her seat in frustration. She took a deep breath then got out and walked towards the front.

The building was painted black and was equal parts eyesore and sort of modern. The glass double doors in the front looked standard, but they were locked.

"Can I help you?" a voice buzzed from somewhere near her. Ella looked around to see where it was. "To your left," the voice helped.

Off to the left of the door, near a potted sago palm tree, Ella spotted the black intercom, which blended right in with the wall. She tried to push a button, but there wasn't one of those either. "Um, hi, yes. I'm Ella; I have an interview today," she tried speaking into it, hoping that no button was needed for her to answer the speaker's question.

A moment passed, then, "Please come in," the voice said, followed by a loud buzzer sound that lasted until Ella pulled the deceptively heavy double doors open. Once she was inside, she felt her world shifting. It was like she'd stepped into the most beautiful office she could imagine.

While the Zeitgeist building was only two stories tall, it was filled with bright light that somehow seemed natural, and there were plants everywhere. Hanging from the ceiling were beautiful crystal chandeliers, and of course there were Mac computers as far as the eye could see. It was like part jungle, part office, part Apple photoshoot.

"Hello..." the voice from the speaker said pulling Ella back into the moment.

"Oh, hi, yes. Hello," Ella tried not to seem flustered as she located where the voice was coming from. Then she noticed a desk to her left. It was empty aside from a giant computer screen, a keyboard, and a mouse. A young, stern-looking woman was sitting there. She had a short, sleek brunette bob with blunt bangs that made her seem too perfect to be a human. Ella secretly looked for a sign that this receptionist was in fact a bot and not a flawless person.

"Hello Ella. You're interviewing with Monica, Jasmine, and Raul today. Please have a seat over there. They'll be right out," the woman said, gesturing to white couch that almost completely blended in with her surroundings. "Do you have any resumes I can give them?" the receptionist asked.

Oh come on, Ella thought to herself, but this place seemed fancy, so she used an excuse that had worked for her in the past. "No, I don't. The email didn't say to bring them, and I try to be environmentally conscious."

"Good for you," the receptionist said in a tone so robotic that it wasn't sarcastic and somehow sincere. Another point for her being a robot, Ella thought.

Before she had a chance to sit down, she heard footsteps coming down the hallway in unison. Ella waited to see who they belonged to. Then suddenly *they* appeared from around the corner.

Monica — who easily could have been a model if she wasn't in her mid-30s, Jasmine — a breathtakingly beautiful woman of indeterminable age, and Raul — a small but bright man who clearly tried to dress like Steve Jobs.

"Hello, this is Ella," the receptionist motioned to Ella.

"Hello! Ella!" Raul exclaimed as he rushed forward to shake her hand. He introduced Monica and Jasmine who were warm but couldn't match Raul's enthusiasm. "Let's give you the tour on the way to our interview room," he said, moving away from the reception area. Ella stole a glance as they walked away, and the receptionist looked tired for a brief moment. One point for being human.

The further they ventured into the facility, the more amazed Ella became. Every person they passed was like the shiniest, most beautiful person Ella had ever seen. So, when they arrived at the conference room for her interview, Ella wasn't surprised in the slightest to see that it had glass windows and a minimalist white boardroom table.

But even in the midst of all of this, Ella still felt a pang of guilt for not telling Zora that she was going on this interview, and not only because she'd obviously need someone to talk about this with later.

The interviewers sat Ella down, and asked her all of the normal interview questions (why do you want this job? Why are you a good fit? How do you feel about working the occasional weekend?) She gave the best possible answers, even if they weren't true. She just wanted something full time that seemed stable. Something where there was room to grow. And if she was being honest, she wanted something that wasn't what she had right now, a sex toy palace.

When Ella thought about it objectively, her job was everything she could have hoped for in a job, including having her best friend there and a super-hot guy she was dating, but it wasn't a job that she got on her own merit, and that feeling never sat right with her. She always wanted something that was *hers*. That she got by being great at what she did every day. And that wasn't how she'd landed her current position. She'd gotten it because she was Zora's friend. Sure, she had a resume that was good enough, but without Zora she'd have never gotten the interview in the first place.

With all of this swirling in Ella's mind as she floated out of the office and back to her car, she wondered if she'd ever be able to work at a place like this. It was so perfect and so... chic. She got in her car and started driving away from the parking lot, trying to imagine if this is what her afternoon commute would look like.

29

When Ella woke up the next morning, she actually felt sick, but knew she couldn't swing two sick days in a row; especially not after she'd called out sick the week before. She convinced herself it was just guilt gnawing at her. She'd lied to Zora the night before when she'd offered to come by Ella's apartment with some soup. The longer this went on, the more Ella wondered to herself why she was so scared to tell Zora about the interview. If they were as good of friends as Ella thought they were, then of course Zora would understand if Ella wanted to work somewhere else, right?

Ella wasn't sure about that, but she knew that she had to get out of bed and start making herself look presentable. She looked at herself in the mirror, expecting the worst after a restless night of sleep but it wasn't as bad as she'd expected. Maybe I should do my skincare routine more often, she thought to herself.

In no mood for a hassle, Ella found the first pair of jeans and a Led Zeppelin t-shirt, then put on some heels so she didn't look too casual, and headed out the door. She fumbled with her keys in the lock which seemed to be jamming more often these days. It was like every time she put the key in, it somehow broke a little more, making it harder to get the key in next time.

Eventually Ella locked her door, walked down the stairs, paying more attention to the keys she'd habitually thrown in her purse, then remembering she needed them to start her car. Suddenly as she rounded the corner towards the front door, she ran right into something hard. Wobbling on her stilettos, Ella fell, tossing her purse and its contents in the air. "What the fuck?!" she said, touching her nose to see if it was bleeding. Mercifully it wasn't.

"Oh my God, I'm so sorry! Here let me help you — Ella?!" the familiar voice sent a shiver down Ella's spine. She didn't want to look up, afraid that her suspicions would be confirmed. But sure enough, Chad's hands were under her arms in a second, helping her back up to her feet. He dropped to his knees, scurrying around to pick up the dropped objects on the floor.

Ella tried to understand what was happening here. Chad was here, in her building. And what had she run into? She looked towards the door to see a man standing there, holding one half of a dresser. The other half Chad had dropped when he picked her up. So that must have been what I ran into, Ella thought to herself.

Feeling a panic attack setting in, Ella finished grabbing her things off the floor and without saying another word to Chad, ran out the front door. "You forgot your —" he yelled after her. "Burn it!" she yelled back. It didn't matter what it was; if Chad had it she didn't need it. She ran to her car, once again fumbling for her keys, pouring out her purse on the hood of her car and frantically realizing they weren't there.

"You forgot your keys," Chad's voice was so close behind her that Ella yelped.

"What the *fuck*, Chad?! What are you trying to do?" she spun around and asked him, swiping the keys from his hand and shoving everything back into her purse again.

"I was just trying to give you your keys back," Chad said casually.

"Well next time you're helping a friend move, stay out of my way," Ella shouted as she got into her car, but he was blocking her way and didn't seem to be moving. She rolled down the passenger window. "Could you *move*?!"

Slowly, a smile spread over Chad's face and it made Ella freeze. Whatever was going to happen next, it wasn't good. "That's just it, El. My friend is helping *me* move. I live here now. I guess that makes us neighbors."

Ella was stunned but tried not to act like it. "Ok congratu-fucking-lations. Now get out of my way."

"Say please," Chad smirked.

".... please," Ella murmured in defeat.

Chad moved aside and Ella pulled out of her parking spot. It took longer than she'd like since she was parallel parked between two cars that had pulled in way too close to hers, compounding the anxiety welling up inside of her. She checked the rear-view mirror as she moved further away from Chad, hoping against hope that he'd have gone back into the apartment, but he was still standing there, waving at her.

30

Ella did the only thing she could think of and called the one person she knew with a biggish home: Mindy. She hadn't seen her new house yet but knew there was no way that Mindy would leave her downtown spot for something smaller.

Mindy's voicemail kicked on; "Hi, you've reached Mindy. I can't come to the phone right now because I'm creating content. Leave a message and I'll call you back when I'm done. Namaste."

Gross, Ella thought to herself. Namaste, from the least authentic person in the world. She hung up and called Mindy again. She did this three more times before Mindy picked up with a hushed whisper. "Um hi— What is it?"

"Mindy! I need to come stay with you!" Ella blurted out.

"Hold on one second," she whispered, then the line went silent.

"Hello?! Mindy?!" Ella asked after a few moments. "Min, did I lose you?"

"I said *hold on*," Mindy said in a sterner tone. Ella kept driving, listening to the silence on the other end for what felt like half an hour but was actually only a few blocks worth of driving time.

"Ok, what do you mean you need to stay with me?" Mindy asked Ella at a normal volume but in a tone that threw Ella off a little bit. Should she still ask her?

"I... I need to stay with you for a while. Is that ok?" Ella decided it might be best to *ask* Mindy instead of *tell* her.

"What's going on, El? Do you need money? I can give you a loan—"

"No!" Ella said a little more forcefully than she meant to. "No. It's not that. I still have my apartment. It's just... well..." Ella couldn't say it. She'd sound crazy saying it, wouldn't she?

"It's just *what*, El?" Mindy asked, making Ella question her request even more.

"It's just that Chad moved into my apartment building." She blurted out, waiting for Mindy's response, which never came, forcing Ella to continue. "I ran into him this morning and he's moving in."

More silence at the other end, then, "Ok, well what do you want me to do about it?"

Ella was shocked that her friend wasn't as alarmed as she was. "Well, I guess I was hoping I could stay with you."

"Stay with me until when? Until you find a new apartment?"

Something inside of Ella snapped. She was angry. "I don't know, Mindy! I'm freaked out, my abusive ex is stalking me, and I just want to know if it's ok to stay with you for a little while."

There was silence on the line. Then finally Mindy let out a long sigh. "Ok El. You can stay here for a few days but that's it. I'll be home around 7 tonight if you want to meet me there then."

"Sure. Thanks, Min," Ella said. Why was her friend only willing to do the bare minimum for her? Couldn't she see how bad this situation could potentially get?

Ella pulled into the parking lot at work and made her way to her desk on autopilot. She hadn't realized she was staring at her screen until she heard Zora's voice behind her. "Still not feeling great?" Zora asked, snapping Ella out of her malaise.

"Zora, I have to talk to you," she told her friend as she stood up and guided them towards the kitchen.

31

Ella decided she couldn't hide her job hunt from Zora any longer. It was too much stress keeping the secret when she had a real stressor in her life now.

They walked to the kitchen. Ella pushed the button on the fancy machine to make an espresso. The coffee maker whirred to life.

"I'm looking for another job," Ella blurted out to Zora, who was standing next to her now.

"Ok. That's fine. Did something happen? Is it Jake? Did he do something to you?" Zora asked, now becoming very protective of her friend.

Ella cut her off, finding brief relief that Zora wasn't outright mad at Ella. "No! No, no. It's nothing like that. It's just, well, I didn't really realize what kind of company this was. And I don't really like the work. It doesn't feel like it's helping me get ahead in my career," Ella felt a weight lift off her with each divulsion. "I know you stuck your neck out for me in helping me get this job and I'm so sorry if I've disappointed you. I'm really grateful and I hope you aren't too mad."

Zora didn't say anything. Instead, she shocked Ella by grabbing her by the shoulders and giving her a big hug. It was the kind of hugs that friends reserve for times like this. She held Ella until the coffee machine flicked off, then let Ella go.

"El, I hope you know me better than that. I'd never disown you, or whatever, because you don't like a job. Work comes and goes, you know? It's totally fine."

Tears started welling in Ella's eyes. "Aren't you going to get your espresso?" Zora asked, still smiling at her friend.

Ella hadn't expected this response from Zora in a million years. Why was that she wondered to herself? Of course, her friend was going to support her. But Ella found it unnerving that she was so convinced Zora would have reacted with anger. Then she flashed back to her conversation with Mindy less than an hour ago. *That's* the type of response Ella was used to from her friends. Maybe when all of this was sorted out, she'd consider spending less time with Mindy.

But for now, Ella grabbed her coffee and turned to Zora. "Then you should know that I wasn't sick yesterday, I was interviewing for a job."

"Do you want the job?"

"Yeah, I think I really do," Ella was relieved at being able to talk about this with someone.

"Then I hope you get it," Zora smiled back. "C'mon. Let's get you back to your desk," she said, starting to leave the kitchen.

"Wait, there's one more thing," Ella said without looking up. "Chad moved into my apartment building."

32

"Um, excuse me?" Zora asked. "Are you sure?"

"Yes! I ran into him when I was leaving this morning. He was moving his stuff in. And then he kinda followed me to my car."

"Hmm... That does sound really odd. What are you going to do about it?" Zora asked.

"Well, that's part of why I need a different job too. I can't afford to get another apartment on what I make here. Mindy said I can stay at her place for a few days while I come up with another plan.

"Good luck with that," Zora quipped. "Ok, well keep me updated on what you decide to do."

"I will. And Zora, thanks for being a good friend."

"Of course," Zora gently cupped her hands around Ella's, which were holding her cup of espresso. "But now I really do have to get to work. Wanna grab lunch?"

"Sure, that'd be great."

Ella gulped down the rest of her espresso, then headed to the machine to make one more before going back to her desk. Even with the Chad situation hanging over her head, she felt confident she'd be able to take it on with her friends by her side.

The rest of the day went by smoothly. Ella found that if she gave her entire focus to her work and didn't let her mind wander, time ticked by a lot faster. And before she knew it, co-workers started packing up for the day, so Ella did too.

She got in her car and drove back to her apartment. But instead of looking for parking this time, she just pulled up to the front, parked in the red zone, and put her hazard lights on. She didn't know which apartment was Chad's and if he had a view of the street, she wanted to get in and out as soon as possible.

Before she even got out of the car, Ella had her door keys in-hand. There was no time to fumble around in her purse for them. She got into the apartment building's main door without a hitch, then navigated her way up the stairs. They seemed much louder than they normally did, as she tried to move as quickly as possible.

Her key slid into her lock, and she slid in, and she rushed in, like she was trying to make sure a dog didn't follow her inside. She closed her door with a little more force than she'd intended, then rested her back against it. She hadn't realized she'd been holding her breath until now. And as she leaned against her door, she heard another door open down the hall.

Was someone looking down the hall? She thought to herself, as she heard a second sound of the opened door closing and footsteps going down the stairs she'd just come up.

Relieved that it was just a neighbor heading out, Ella's attention snapped back to the task at hand and ran to her bedroom. She started shoving things into a suitcase, even grabbing a few of her wardrobe staples out of her dirty clothes pile.

Next, she made her way to the bathroom, taking her toothbrush and a few necessities from her medicine cabinet. She paused for a moment, looking at her reflection. The face that looked back at her seemed frightened, and this wasn't the face she was used to seeing. But there wasn't time for another pep talk. That would have to wait until she was safely at Mindy's house.

Looking over the rest of her apartment to see if she'd forgotten any other essentials and deciding she hadn't, Ella once again got her keys ready and started to open the door. She wasn't sure why but something told her not to go out yet. She looked out of the peephole and didn't see anything. She listened for a second longer but heard only silence. Deciding she was being paranoid, she opened her door and maneuvered her suitcase into the hallway as quietly as she could.

Getting down the stairs without making noise was another issue though. She held her breath and did the only thing she could think of to get out of there as fast as possible. After looking around to make sure there was no one who could see her, Ella barreled down the stairs, her much-too-heavy suitcase thumping hard on every step, then rolled it out the front door, and shoved it into her back seat.

Ella didn't look back to see if anyone had heard her and come outside to see what the noise was. If anyone had, she didn't want to know. She just started her car, put it in Drive, and headed for the hills.

33

Mindy's new house was even more impressive than Ella had imagined. It wasn't a mansion or anything, but anyone their age having a cute little bungalow in the Hollywood Hills felt almost regal.

There were no cars in the driveway, so Ella texted Mindy.

ELLA: Hey! I'm here. Is anyone home?

The response was immediate.

MINDY: I'm tied up with something at work. But Creel should be there. Knock and he'll let you in. He knows you're coming.
ELLA: Okay thanks! See you soon.

The idea of having to spend time with Creel was almost bad enough for Ella to stay in the car until Mindy got home, but that would make things awkward considering she'd be staying here for a while. So, she got out, grabbed her bag and walked up to the large wooden door.

It was much larger than she'd thought from the driveway, maybe almost 20ft high, and gave off a tiki vibe. Even though Creel was on the other side of the door, there was something that felt peaceful about the home. Maybe it was knowing that there was no way Chad could find her here.

She knocked on the door and waited. No answer. So, she knocked a little louder. Still nothing. Maybe Creel wasn't home after all.

Ella started putting her bag back into her car when she heard what sounded like chimes coming from the backyard. She walked around the side and saw Creel sitting in the middle of a grass yard, surrounded by crystal singing bowls. He was tapping them in rhythm, swirling the crystal stick around them so they echoed and reverberated. He seemed in his own world and Ella didn't want to disturb him, so she walked back to her car.

"Ella?" he said, abruptly stopping the sound coming from the bowls by placing his hand on top of them.

She turned around slowly, giving him a sheepish smile. "Hi, yeah it's me."

"I thought I'd sensed an energetic disturbance," he said, looking as smug as always. She disliked him more each time they crossed paths.

"Well Mindy isn't home but you're welcome to come inside," he said, getting up, clearly over whatever it was he'd been doing before.

"Ok thanks. Those are some nice, uh, bowls there. What do they do?" she tried to make conversation with this man who she had absolutely nothing in common with.

"Oh, those are crystal singing bowls. I was giving myself a sound bath. The acoustics in this yard are perfect for beta wave frequencies. It's the perfect pick-me-up in the afternoon."

Ella didn't know what any of that meant but she played along, following him into the house through the backyard. "Well, I'm sorry that I interrupted your bath."

"No apologies needed. Come on, I'll make us some green juice," Creel said, ushering her into the house.

To Creel's credit, the backyard did feel very Zen. It was symmetrical with sparse decorating; clearly it was meant to be a place of chill instead of a place to socialize. She stepped through the sliding glass door and into the house, where the tiki Zen decor continued. There were crystals, jade statuettes, and natural wood throughout the open floor plan. It was obviously more Creel's style than Mindy's, but the longer Ella was here the more she thought she could get used to it. There was a calming energy in the place.

"Did you bring a bag?" Creel asked, starting to put some celery and cucumbers into the juicer.

"Oh my god. I completely forgot. It's in the car. I'll run out and get it," Ella said, thankful to have something to do to kill the time until Mindy got there. She walked outside and her phone buzzed. It was her landlord.

"Hello?" she answered, hearing loud sounds coming from the other end. Her landlord yelled, "Hi! Ella? This is your landlord, Frank."

"Hi, yes I have your number saved Frank. What's going on?" she asked, wanting him to get to the point.

"Ella, there's a burst pipe in the apartment above yours. We're going to need access for a few days — probably a week to fix it. Do you have somewhere you can stay?"

"A burst pipe? How bad is the damage to my stuff?"

"It seems like it's just in the bathroom for now and we turned the water off to the building so your property should be fine. But we will need to go in and out for a few days, so it won't be ideal for you to stay here."

Ella wasn't thrilled with the idea of strangers going in and out of her apartment and it being exposed, but at least she'd already taken her valuables with her.

"Yeah, that's fine. I have somewhere I can stay," she said. "Does this mean you'll prorate my rent?" she asked.

"Sure, we can talk about that," he said, and Ella knew she would likely end up paying the same as usual, but it was worth a try. "Ok, gotta go. I'll call when I have an update."

"Ok, thanks, Frank," she said and hung up.

34

Ella grabbed her bag, looking at it a little differently now that it was potentially her only possessions that hadn't been damaged. In the few interactions she'd had with Frank, she knew he'd try to downplay anything that could cost him more money. She also felt a little guilty that she was happy to have a real reason why she needed to stay here for a while besides her Chad paranoia. Before, Ella sensed that Mindy was hesitant about having Ella stay with her and Creel, but now she'd have to let her.

As Ella was locking her car door, Mindy's car pulled into the driveway. She waved from the driver's seat as she pulled next to Ella.

"Hey! Have you been outside this whole time?" she asked, grabbing her purse and making her way around the car to Ella.

"No! No, I accidentally interrupted Creel's backyard sound bath then came back out to grab my bag."

Mindy looked worried. "Oh no. I bet he didn't like that one bit."

"He was polite about it," Ella dodged, not trying to start anything her first hour here.

"Well, let's go inside then," Mindy led the way. "What do you think of the place?"

"It's amazing! Very Zen."

"That's all Creel's doing," Mindy confirmed Ella's suspicions.

"Is that my Min-Min?" Creel said, emerging from the kitchen with three green juices on a bamboo tray.

Ella took her juice and tried to ignore the baby talk greetings they gave each other. She walked back into the kitchen and sat down at the table, dropping her bag next to her.

"Oh, Ella, can you put your bag in the guest room? We don't like a lot of clutter. It disrupts the feng shui," Mindy crooned at her, with a big fake smile.

"Sure! I'm sorry, I just didn't want to break up your love fest," Ella said, her expression matching Mindy's.

"Ok great, so, the guest room is just down that hall on the right. There's a bathroom too so you can make yourself at home."

"But not too much at home!" Creel shouted down the hall after her. "Just kidding," he added after a long pause, letting her know that he indeed was not kidding. Ella would never understand why Mindy was with a poser like him, trying to be the quintessential LA guy. But then again, she'd never understood why she'd dated a guy like Chad either.

She walked in the guest room and instantly felt like she was in a chic B&B. The decor matched the rest of the house, and there was a towel set neatly folded at the end of the bed. Ella guessed that Mindy left it like this all of the time because she couldn't have done this while she was at work, and there was no way Creel was going to do anything to make her feel welcome.

After she poked around and got out her essentials, Ella started back down the hall toward the kitchen. She heard

Mindy and Creel talking in low whispers and stopped to eavesdrop.

"She is absolutely killing my vibe. I can't believe you agreed to let her stay without asking me," Creel said.

"I know honey, she's just going through something right now. It's only a few days."

"When is she ever not going through something? It's like she fabricates a crisis out of thin air every week."

"Wow, she really has messed with your vibes. This is some strong negativity you're expressing."

"I know. So just imagine how much worse I'll be in a few days."

Were they being serious, Ella wondered to herself?

Maybe now was the time to let them know about the burst pipe, then watch both of their faces crumble when they realized she wasn't *fabricating a crisis*, or whatever.

Ella quickened her stride so they could hear her coming and cut their not-so-private conversation off. "Wow, you aren't going to believe what happened."

"I'm quite sure we won't," Creel sighed, and Mindy shot him a look, urging him to shut up.

"What is it, El?"

"The pipes burst in my apartment, so I can't stay there for a week." She watched a flicker of dread flash over both of their expressions.

"Oh no, that's awful. Is your stuff ok?" Mindy asked, trying to seem more concerned than inconvenienced.

"There's no way of knowing," Ella said, loving every minute of this. "So, I wanted to say double thank you for letting me stay here. There's no way I could afford a hotel, so I'd be out in the cold otherwise." Ella said, guilting them into letting her stay there.

There was silence, then Mindy stood and walked over to Ella, giving her a big, comforting hug. "Of course, you can stay here for as long as you need to."

"Thanks, Min. You're the best."

Ella felt a little bad about how much she loved watching Creel try to not melt down in the corner. "I'll be in the Zen Garden," he abruptly announced and walked outside.

"You have a Zen Garden?" Ella asked Mindy.

"Yeah, Creel likes to rake sand when he's anxious," Mindy said, and Ella detected a slight hint of annoyance in her tone. Could she finally be over Creel's act too? Then she quickly added, "There's a lot of studies that explain why it's beneficial."

"I'll have to look it up," Ella said, knowing she had no intention of doing so. "So, do you eat dinner around here or just drink juice?"

"Dinner! Yes, let's find something to make. Maybe we'll just have some wine and pasta like old times," Mindy said, and for a second Ella saw a flicker of the old friend she'd grown up with, before Mindy had tried to fit a certain mold.

"Sounds good to me," Ella said, following her friend to the kitchen.

175

35

Surprisingly, the week at Mindy's went by almost without a hitch. There were a few tense discussions between Ella and Creel, but overall, Ella's schedule made it easy to stay out of their way.

Towards the end of the week when Ella hadn't heard back from her landlord, curiosity got the best of her, and she drove over to the apartment. Tension rose in her with each block.

From the outside, the building looked like it always did. A basic facade, clean but plain. And quiet. Ella was always surprised how quiet the building was for how many people lived there.

She once again parallel parked on the curb outside. Before walking inside, Ella took a deep breath, gave herself a silent pep talk and walked in.

Immediately she was assaulted by a thin cloud of dust drifting down from the floor above. Her floor. There wasn't anything that sounded like construction though. A few clangs but largely quiet.

Ella walked up the stairs, preparing herself to see an apartment completely in shambles. As she approached, she saw that her front door was flung wide open. Anyone passing by would be able to walk in, take a look around, and maybe steal a souvenir or two. She was pushing down the urge to yell at whoever was making the clanging noises coming from her unit.

She walked in. "Hello?!"

The clanging stopped. "Oh, hey. Ella is that you?" she heard the voice of her landlord Frank. He emerged from the bathroom covered in sweat and dust clinging to the tips of his hair.

"Hey, yeah. I see you're still working here. Is it just you doing the repairs?"

Frank was average in just about every way, so whenever he got the chance to talk himself up, he did. Standing a little taller Frank explained, "Oh, no the construction crew is just out to lunch. I like to get my hands dirty once in a while so I'm helping pick up the slack."

"Ok, gotcha. Well, can I ask why my door is wide open? Anyone could just walk in here and take something while you're not looking," she tried not to sound as angry as she was.

Frank was defensive. "Do you think I let criminals live in this building?"

"The first step of a crime is finding an opportunity. And I'd say you've given them a pretty big one."

"Ok, I'll make sure to close it from now on. That sound ok?" Frank was not in the mood for an argument. Ella hadn't had many conversations with him, just the occasional repair, half of which she had to haggle with him over.

"That's fine. Thanks. So, when do you think you'll be done?"

"Well, we finished the apartment upstairs and that tenant is back in his unit, so I'd say we could be done here by the end of the day. Maybe midday tomorrow depending on how long it takes to clean all of this up," he gestured around to the tarps on her floor and pointed back toward the bathroom.

"Great. I'm just going to grab something from my room then head out, but can you please let me know when you're done? You didn't return my last three calls."

"I didn't?" Frank reached for his phone, trying to act innocent. "Wow, sorry about that. I'll be sure to call you."

"Thanks," Ella said flatly and headed to her room.

"I'm going to run out to my truck to get a tool, so I'll give you some privacy," he said, unbuckling his tool belt and laying it outside the bathroom door.

"Uh, ok cool. Thanks," Ella wasn't sure what he thought that she needed privacy for, but she had to admit that it was nice to be alone in her apartment again, even if it was only for a few minutes.

She walked into her room and looked at the pile of dirty clothes in the corner. She wasn't excited to get back to the reality of living here again. But at least she'd have a semi-new bathroom now. There really was nothing Ella needed to grab from her room, so instead she did a once over to make sure there was nothing glaring that had been stolen. Then walked back out to the main room where she was more than annoyed to find Frank had not closed the front door. There it was, flung wide open.

She grabbed a post-it note and wrote, "CLOSE THE DOOR!" on it, and slapped it on the front of her door, right in the middle where Frank couldn't possibly miss it. As she pulled the door shut and took out her keys to lock it, she heard someone coming down the stairs.

"Ella?" Chad's voice came from the staircase and sent a chill through her. "We've got to stop meeting like this," he joked.

36

Ella finished locking her door before turning around. She tried to put on a fake smile but couldn't manage, hoping that at the very least she didn't look as frozen with fear as she felt.

"Hey Chad," she hoped she sounded calm.

"So, you're the person below me who had to leave for a week too, huh?" he still made no indication that he was going to stop having this conversation and continue on his way.

"Uh, yeah I guess so." There was nothing Ella wanted less than to let Chad know which apartment was hers, though she guessed he already figured it out from the mailboxes. Had he *wanted* to move above her? Had he intentionally caused this leaky pipe to somehow gain access to her apartment? Ella knew she was dangerously close to spiraling into irrationality. Calm down, she told herself. As she did, he appeared to get the hint that she didn't want to talk.

"Ok well I guess I'll see you around then," Chad said, checking his smartwatch. "Actually, I'm headed out on a lunch date. It's with your friend Trix. I hope that's ok. I figured she wouldn't have said ok if you weren't cool with it."

She wasn't sure why he was telling her this but was even more confused about why Trix would do this. It wasn't like she and Trix were the best of friends, but she'd told Trix most of her horror stories about Chad, hadn't she? She hadn't told her about the mysterious video though.

"Oh, uh, yeah. Yeah, she told me. Totally cool," Ella lied. She wanted to get out of there but didn't want to walk down the stairs with him. "You know what, I forgot something inside. Have fun with Trix," Ella said, fumbling to unlock her door.

"I'm sure I will," Chad said but didn't move from his spot on the stairs.

"Oh, I see you've met our new tenant Chad," Ella had never been so happy to hear Frank's voice in her life.

"Hey Frank," Chad said, waving at their landlord who was climbing the stairs with a considerable amount of effort.

"Yeah, actually Ella and I go way back. We were just catching up."

"Wow! Small world," Frank smiled. "See Ella? I told you I only let good people into this building."

You have no idea, Ella thought to herself as she disappeared into her apartment and shut the door without saying a word to either of them.

37

Ella waited in her room for a few minutes until she was sure that Chad had time to drive away. Frank was already making noise in the bathroom. She grabbed her purse and walked toward the door.

"Bye Frank. Please don't forget to—"

"—Answer your calls, I know," he cut her off.

"Actually, I was going to say close the door, but yes, please also answer my call so I know when I can come back. By the way, you said I was able to take 25% off my rent, right? Since I couldn't be here for a week?"

"Still working out the math. I'll talk to you later," he avoided the question.

Ella left and went out to her car, relieved that there was no sign of Chad anywhere. She debated whether she should text or call Trix. Since she was likely already on her way to the lunch date, Ella decided a call would be the quickest way to get a hold of her.

The phone kept ringing, and Ella thought she was too late, that Trix was already at lunch with Chad. But a groggy voice came through on the other end.

"Hello?" Trix said, clearly woken up by the phone call.

"Hey Trix, it's Ella. Are you… are you asleep?" Why would she be asleep if she had a lunch date? Had Chad been lying to get Ella wound up? Surely he'd assume that she'd call her friend.

"Well, I was asleep until you called. What's up?"

"Oh um, well, I guess this is a little awkward then."

"Great. An awkward wakeup call. My favorite thing. Hey, what time is it anyway?"

"It's just past noon. That's why I'm calling. I ran into my ex Chad — long story — but he said you two were meeting up for a lunch date."

"Oh shit! That's right!" Trix was suddenly awake and alert. Ella could hear rustling sounds coming through the other end of the phone.

"Ok yeah, well, I just wanted to tell you that you shouldn't go," Ella blurted out, and the noise on the other end calmed a little.

"Look, El, I thought you were super over him. I wouldn't have said yes if I thought you still had a thing for him," Trix said.

"No!" Ella exclaimed a little too forcefully. "No, I'm not into him. It's just, well. Trix, I think Chad is dangerous."

"Yeah, I know. I remember those stories you told us. But if I'm being honest, he just seems like your classic awkward guy."

"That's why I thought too, but I think it's deeper than that, Trix. I don't want you to get hurt, that's all."

"No need to worry about that, hon. He was in the club last night, paid for a few dances, and asked me to lunch. That's all. I'm just trying to get a free meal or two out of this. I'm not trying to marry the guy."

"Ok well as long as you know what you're getting into," Ella was still hesitant about her friend going out with him.

"Don't worry, lady. If I wasn't careful in my line of work, I'd have died ten times by now. At least! But hey, I gotta go. You think I should order a bison burger or the crab cakes?"

"I don't know. Whichever has the better sauce."

"Good point. Ok, see ya, El."

"Bye Trix. Text me when you're home safe ok?"

"El…"

"Just do it, please. It'll take you 10 seconds and will make me feel a lot better."

"Ok you've got it."

Ella hung up, relieved that Trix wasn't actually interested in Chad. There was no way Ella was jealous, was there?

38

When Ella got back to Mindy's later that afternoon, she heard some yelling coming from inside. She paused briefly at the front door to try and see if she could hear what the commotion was about. The thick wood door made it difficult to hear anything.

Then suddenly she heard her name out of nowhere. "Ella," it was Mindy's voice. "Ella, we can see you listening at the door," the voice continued.

Ella looked down and saw one of those video camera systems discreetly installed in the doorframe. Very clever, she thought to herself, and opened the door. She was greeted with her suitcase sitting in the front foyer, Mindy standing next to it, and Creel slinking off back towards the kitchen.

"What's going on?" Ella said hesitantly.

"Hey girl, I hate to do this, but you can't stay here anymore," a touch of exasperation was evident in Mindy's tone.

"Is everything ok?" Ella asked, not sure why there was such an abrupt need for her to leave.

"No yeah, no it's not. Creel just feels like his energy is totally off with you here and is nervous it's affecting his meetings. I've packed up your stuff for you." Mindy lowered her voice before saying, "I'm really sorry about this."

"Oh, um. Ok then. Can I go take one look around to make sure you didn't miss anything?"

In the same low tone, Mindy said, "Actually I don't think that's a good idea. Look, I'll call you, ok? We'll find a time for you to swing by." Mindy's look was pleading for Ella to leave but it all felt so rushed and sudden.

"Ok, sure. But hey, Min, you'd tell me if you weren't ok right?" Ella asked, suddenly worried about her friend.

"Definitely. It'll be fine," Mindy flashed Ella a smile as she ushered her out of the front door and back towards the driveway. "Hopefully your apartment is done by now."

"Yeah, I hope so too."

Once she got in the car, Ella called Frank. He picked up on the second ring. "Hey Ella. See? I answered your call just like you asked."

"You sure did," Ella said, trying to hide her annoyance at how proud he was of himself for doing the bare minimum. "Hey, um, is the apartment ready? I'm going to need to come back tonight."

"Well, the repairs are done, but it still needs to be cleaned up. I was going to suggest tomorrow would be better."

"I don't really have a choice, Frank. So, I'm coming back tonight. Don't worry about sending in a crew tomorrow, I'll clean it up myself. Unless you want to put me up in a hotel for the night." Ella was secretly glad tomorrow was Saturday so she could spend the day cleaning and settling back in.

"Ok well, if you're sure..." It was obvious Frank didn't want to have to pay the crew to come in just to clean up nor for a hotel room.

"I'm positive," Ella said, feeling a sense of relief at getting her own space back. But that was quickly crowded out when she remembered Chad was living right above her. She didn't want his energy that close to her. Maybe I *have* been spending too much time with Creel, Ella thought.

She hung up with Frank and realized that Trix had never texted to say she got home safe.

ELLA: Trix, you get home safe?

Ella put her phone in the seat next to her, glancing at it every few seconds. Two red lights later, the bubbles indicating that Trix was typing popped up.

TRIX: Yeah. A great lunch. Hey, maybe give the guy a second chance? He still seems like he's pretty into you.

What the hell had Chad told her, Ella wondered.

ELLA: Hmm... let's talk when you get a chance. Maybe grab a drink before you go to work?

No response.

ELLA: I'll get the first round.

The bubbles popped up again.

TRIX: I'm in. Just meet me at the bar next to the club at 7.

Ella had been looking forward to settling into her apartment after what felt like the longest week of her life, but she had to know what Chad said to Trix. The longer she waited to find out the more she knew she'd obsess about it. There was no chance she was ever trusting Chad again, but she wanted to know what charm he'd turned on that made Trix of all people trust him. She didn't like that he could potentially be turning her friends on her.

She lugged her suitcase up the stairs, trying to be quiet, but also feeling too emotionally drained to care if she ran into Chad at this point.

When she got to her door, she found that it had been left unlocked. For a moment, she felt rage toward Frank brewing, until she noticed a little pin poking out from the lock. It was thin, but unmistakable. Someone had picked her lock.

39

Ella peered up and down her hall, looking for any sign that something was amiss, but all was as it should be. She removed the pin and grabbed her pepper spray before entering her apartment.

With the spray at-ready, Ella inspected every nook and cranny, making sure there was no one in any of the closets or under and furniture. Once she felt satisfied that she was alone, she locked her door and put a chair up against it so that no one could get it.

She poured a big glass of wine to take the edge off and drank it much faster than she should have. It was almost time to meet Trix, so she ordered a rideshare and changed her clothes. By the time she was ready, the car was outside.

Before leaving the apartment though, she set a booby trap, so she'd know if someone had gone in there. She plucked a strand of hair from her head and taped it across the door so it would break if someone came in, like she'd seen in one of the early James Bond movies. If it was good enough for 007 it had to be for her. Ella carefully closed the door, making sure both the tape and the hair were intact.

Once inside the car she started Googling laws about owning a gun in California. It seemed like it would take a long time, which in theory she agreed with, but she needed something to keep her safe right now. Trix will know what to do, Ella thought to herself, adding it to the list of things they needed to talk about.

40

Ella got to the bar next to the strip club already feeling a little buzzed. Trix was at the bar in a t-shirt and jeans, talking with the bartender. Aside from a few seedy folks in the dark corners, they were the only people there.

Trix waved Ella over and told the bartender, "Next round is on her." Ella was always amazed at how unashamed Trix was when it came to getting other people to pay for things. Then again, if she had to take off her clothes for a paycheck, she'd probably feel pretty attached to her money too.

"What'll it be?" the bartender asked. "Whatever your house red is, please."

"I'll have a tequila rocks. If I have wine this early I'll be bloated by the time I have to take the stage," Trix joked half-heartedly.

"Ok, let's cut to the chase," Ella didn't want to waste any time if Trix had to go to work soon. "Why was Chad talking about me?"

"Geeze, no messing around with you today. Ok, yeah. He just mentioned that he'd moved into your same building and what a coincidence it was. To be honest, it wasn't so much *what* he said but *how* he talked about you. Like, that guy clearly still loves you," Trix said. That was not what Ella wanted to hear but she'd already assumed as much.

"Don't you find that creepy though? That he'd love me so much he'd follow me around after we broke up and would move into my building?" she wasn't ready to tell Trix about the video because if she was honest with herself, she was still in denial over it, and had yet to confirm it was Chad who filmed it and sent it. If she brought it up, she risked sounding crazier than she already felt, and she couldn't risk that with her next request from Trix.

"Well, the building thing sounds like a genuine coincidence. You have one of the few rent-controlled spots in the city. Everyone wants to live there."

It was true she lived in a pretty sought-after place. "Ok well, what else did you talk about? How'd the date go?"

"It was fine, a normal date. But no matter what we talked about he kept coming back to you somehow," Trix said, downing the glass of tequila and motioning for one more.

"That's *weird*, Trix. I don't know how you don't see that?" Ella was feeling frustrated that people kept giving Chad the benefit of the doubt. He was stalking her and no one was even trying to see her side of it because he was such a pathetic person.

"Ella look, Chad is a weird dude, but not dangerous. Just a weird, lonely dude who probably doesn't get many girls. That's why guys like him go to strip clubs."

"No, *he* went to *your* strip club to try and get close to me through you," Ella felt frustration rising and took a swig of her wine. It tasted like horrible house wine, but she was already buzzed so she didn't care. The bottle probably cost less at the store than they charged this one glass. "Why can't you see that?"

"Can you hear yourself?" Trix asked, causing Ella to pause. She knew she sounded crazy. But that's exactly what Chad wanted. She decided to change the subject.

"Ok I need your help with something else," Ella said, letting her frustration flow away for the moment. "I know you just said I'm crazy, but something *did* happen today." Trix urged Ella on with her look. "They've been fixing a pipe in my bathroom for a week. When I got home today, there was a pin in the lock, like someone had picked it."

Trix looked suspiciously at Ella and sipped her tequila.

"I know this sounds, well, crazy, but I know what I saw."

"Was anything missing?" Trix asked.

"No, not that I could tell."

"Maybe one of the workers forgot something and just needed to grab it really quick."

"Yeah sure, I guess that makes sense." Ella felt foolish that she hadn't thought of that before. "But that's not what my question is. I just don't feel safe there anymore, but I'm too broke at the moment to move. So I'm thinking I might want to get a gun." Ella couldn't believe she'd said that out loud.

Trix looked serious. "Ok, and why are you telling me?"

"Well, I looked at the laws in California and it'll take weeks for me to get approved. And what if I don't have weeks? What if whoever it was is in there right now waiting for me to come back?"

"Uh huh… and what do you want me to do about it?" Trix's expression was growing darker by the moment.

"Well, I thought you might know someone who could maybe get me a gun? You know, *outside of official channels*?" Ella felt like a corny dork saying it like that, but what else was it called?

Trix leaned in, and Ella matched her body language. "Look, El. Guys who sell illegal guns are not to be fucked with. It'll cost you more than to buy a regular gun, and you've got to be serious about it. You understand, right?"

Ella felt herself involuntarily gulp. "Yeah, ok, I get it. But I need one. So how much do you think it'll be?"

Trix exhaled and leaned back. "Probably more than you have. Around $700." She was right; that was more than Ella had. "Look, I can loan you the money. Just give me like $100 a month or something."

"Seriously?" Ella asked. Trix was different from the rest of them in many ways, but if any of them needed something, she was always down to help.

"Of course," Trix smiled, and finished her second tequila. She got up to leave. "Look, I've got to go to work, but just be ready tomorrow night, ok? But you can't back out of this once it's in motion. I'll meet you behind the club at 3am tomorrow night."

Ella got up and gave her a big hug. "Thanks, Trix," she said, relieved that even if her friends didn't believe her, they supported her.

Trix left and Ella sat back down. "Hey, she didn't close out of her tab. Are you paying for her?" the bartender asked.

Ella laughed, "Sure."

41

Never in a million years would Ella have guessed that she'd be buying a gun in some back-alley deal, but she wasn't sure how else she could stay safe in this situation. On her ride home from the bar, she opened up an incognito tab and searched "Penalty for owning an illegal gun." There were hundreds of results.

The first one was from a legal blog, explaining that penalties were different depending on the state. The second link was a recent news story about how many illegal guns were on the street in Chicago. As she was about to click on the third one, "6 Reasons Buying Illegal Guns Will Land You in Prison," her phone buzzed.

It was Jake. Everything felt so hectic lately that she'd almost forgotten about him.

JAKE: Hey. What are you up to?

She looked at the clock on the top of her screen; it was 8:15pm.

ELLA: Just heading home from the bar. You?

What could he want? They'd barely talked since their last date, and she'd been under the impression that he wasn't interested in her anymore since it had ended so awkwardly. She hadn't seen him around the office either and assumed he'd been avoiding her.

JAKE: Just got back in town. Do you feel like heading back to the bar?

He hadn't mentioned leaving for anywhere the last time they talked. Ella's curiosity was piqued.

ELLA: Sounds mysterious. Sure! Where should I reroute my driver to?
JAKE: A driver? Fancy.
ELLA: It sounds better than "my rideshare."
JAKE: Yes it does. You pick the place and send me the address.

Ella wanted nothing more than to go home, so she told the driver to take her there and sent Jake the address for the bar across the street. The worst thing that could happen is they'd run into Chad and since that already happened, she figured she'd save herself the money for a ride home and go there.

Besides, who knew where the night would lead. Ella wasn't sure if it was the wine she'd been drinking all night, but she felt dangerous, in a cool way. She didn't care if her insane ex saw her out with the hottest man in the world for a *second* time. She was buying an illegal gun the next night. She was living life on the edge.

The car pulled up to her apartment building. She got out and crossed the street. For a fleeting second she wondered if Chad was anywhere near her, lurking in the dark. But thinking that a man would be waiting around for hours to see her get back felt nuts even to her.

So, Ella held her head up high, crossed the street, and walked into the bar. She was immediately greeted by the sight of Chad sitting in a corner booth.

42

She didn't think he hadn't noticed her, so Ella skulked behind a wall and towards one of the attached rooms on the opposite side of the building. Luckily this was one of those bars with lots of inexplicable walls that ruined the flow of the place but offered lots of spots to disappear.

ELLA: When you come in, go down the hall to the right. I'm in the back room.
JAKE: Back room? Sounds mysterious. I'm on my way.

The only problem with being in the back room was that the server was always slow to notice anyone at the table. So, Ella was shocked when a nice-looking woman her age came over to her.

"What can I get for you?" she asked.

"Um, wow. This was fast! I'm not really sure. I guess two Old Fashioneds. Men like those, right?"

"If I knew what men liked, I'd be married to a rich one by now."

"Ok, then bring me the opposite of what you'd order for a man," Ella tentatively joked, hoping the server would understand her humor.

"Ha! Good one," the server laughed. Ella was relieved. "I'll be right back."

Ella looked at her phone out of habit, but there were no new notifications. She lost herself aimlessly scrolling through Instagram, still feeling buzzed from the drinks she'd already had.

"Anyone sitting here?" she heard Jake's familiar voice and her attention came back to the room. He still looked as handsome as ever, in a simple t-shirt and jeans. How is it that men can look so good in those two things, she asked herself?

"Oh, yeah, I'm actually meeting someone here. I haven't seen him in so long though that I've almost forgotten what he looks like," she joked, impressed that she was able to act so cool around him.

By chance, the server walked up at that moment with two of the brightest, most fruity drinks Ella had even seen in her life and was slightly mortified.

"What are *these*?" Jake was smiling ear to ear looking at the concoctions, and Ella realized she'd never seen him with this expression before. Was it delight? How often did anyone feel delight?

"*These*," the server said, "are the opposite of what I'd order for a man," she said and winked at Ella, who felt her cheeks flush.

"Oh, wait, were you actually expecting someone else?" Jake questioned Ella, delight fading to confused bemusement. But he clearly had no intention of leaving no matter her answer because he gently took one of the rainbow drinks and started inspecting it.

The glass was a giant bowl with different colorful layers and so many cocktail umbrellas that it was hard to find the straw.

"Enjoy," the server said and walked away.

Ella looked at their drinks apologetically. "I didn't know what you'd want to drink. She said she always orders the wrong thing for her dates, so I asked for the opposite of whatever she usually orders."

Jake gave a quick, genuine laugh then raised his cup — which took two hands to hold — and they both said "cheers" to nothing in particular and took long sips.

"Wow, that is strong," Ella said.

"You know," Jake started, "It turns out this is *exactly* what I wanted to drink right now."

"Don't patronize me," she shot him a look.

"Oh, I'm not kidding. After the week I've had, a strong fruity drink with you feels like a vacation."

Ella was relieved that he'd mentioned *his* week so she didn't have to talk about hers first. "Do tell," she encouraged.

"One second," he took a long drink from his straw, which apparently changed color as the frosty liquid flowed through it.

They spent the next hour chatting about what had happened in their lives over the last week. Jake explained that he'd gone back home to Wyoming to help his parents take care of some legal issues that had come up with their family ranch. They lived near Jackson Hole and a real estate developer made them think he'd bought the rights to their land, which it turned out wasn't the truth at all.

Ella talked about her burst pipe and what it was like staying with Mindy and Creel. She left out the parts about Chad moving into her building and her job interview. If she was barely able to tell Zora about the interview there was no way that she was going to tell Jake.

Both of their glasses were empty and they were feeling a serious buzz. The server came back. "Another round?" she asked. They both answered with an emphatic "no."

"Can I just get a glass of red wine?" Ella asked, knowing that she had probably already drunk too much for one night, but she always felt weird not ordering something. Like if she started drinking water the night was somehow over, and it wasn't even 10pm yet. "And water!" she added for good measure.

"That sounds great. I'll have the same thing," Jake said, and it surprised Ella a little. She'd never guessed that he was a wine guy. Then again, she hadn't thought of him as a fruity drink guy either. While they waited for their wine and water, Jake moved closer to Ella. He smelled clean, like a shower scent, but it wasn't artificial. He actually just smelled that way. She tried to not take an awkwardly deep breath, but it was hard.

"Hey, so I wanted to ask you —" Jake started, but he was cut off by the one sound in the world Ella never wanted to hear again.

"Oh my God. I can't believe this is happening again." It was Chad. He was smiling and hovering over their table.

Ella audibly groaned. *This can't be happening.* She'd known there was a risk they'd run into him since she'd seen him earlier. But she was so certain that she was far enough out of the way that he'd never find them unless he was actively walking around, looking for her. That was a bet that had backfired.

Jake looked at Ella with something between accusation and inquisition, but he still subconsciously pulled his arm around her, protecting her from Chad.

"Stop following us, Chad," Ella said. She didn't want Jake to think that she and him were friends in any sense of the word.

"Following you? We just keep running into each other, babe. Maybe the universe wants us to be together or something." His laugh made every muscle in Ella's body tense.

Ella was trying to conjure up some cutting response when Jake said, "Or maybe it doesn't." He stared hard at Chad and it was clear that for a moment he was shaken off whatever game he was playing.

Chad stared hard at Jake before turning what was now a steely gaze on Ella. "See you later, El," he said before walking off.

Jake's grip on Ella eased and the mood shifted. It was no longer heavy, but it wasn't light either. Ella mentally begged for the server to come back with their drinks so she had something to fidget with or do to stave off the wave of fear she felt coming on.

"What did he mean he'd see you later?" Jake asked. He wasn't mad, and Ella was beyond thankful for that. He was just curious.

"I didn't want to bring this up," Ella started, but Jake's expression didn't change. "Chad moved into my building."

"He *what*?!" Jake exclaimed, leaning back toward her, which made Ella send up a second round of thanks.

"Ok, that's what I'm saying! All of my friends think I'm overreacting."

"Even Z?!"

"Yes, even her," Ella realized too late she'd thrown her friend under the bus.

"Have they met this guy? He's a Level 5 creeper."

"YES! Thank you!" Ella felt an overwhelming wave of relief wash over her. For the first time in weeks she didn't feel insane. She felt like her concerns were validated, but she wondered why it was only Jake who was validating them. Why couldn't her friends see Chad the same way Jake did?

"So what are you going to do?" the question caught her off guard.

"What do you mean?"

"Well, you can't keep living there, obviously."

She wasn't sure how much she should tell him. "To be honest, I'm not sure. I'm too broke to move out, and there have been some weird things that have happened since he moved in."

Jake moved closer, once again acting protective. "What kind of weird things?"

She explained the pipe and the pin in her door. *Should she show him the video?* She asked herself. It was so unsettling and weird. Would it scare him off? But at the same time, he was the only person in the world who believed her right now, and more than anything she wanted someone to make her feel like she wasn't completely losing it.

"And there's one more thing," she pulled out her phone and hit play on the video.

"What the fuck?" he asked, bewildered and unsettled, which was exactly how she felt.

"I don't know. I mean, it's clearly me. And I think Chad sent it, but I have no way of knowing."

"Ella, you can't stay there," he said.

"I know."

"Stay with me tonight?" he reached out and took her hand as he said it. She looked at his perfect face, his perfectly concerned eyes, and wondered how such an imperfectly perfect moment could be happening to her.

She nodded in response, just as the server came around the corner with their drinks. "Whoops! Sorry, I'm interrupting something," she said, quickly setting down the drinks.

"I want to close out, please," Ella said a little too urgently.

"Ok, no problem," the server said, picking up on the urgency. "Be back in a minute."

Jake and Ella looked at their glasses of wine, clinked glasses and chugged.

She finished first. "Classy," he said once he caught up.

"I'm under a lot of stress," she cracked in a valley girl voice, hoping to lighten the mood.

The server kept her word and returned quickly with the check. Jake called a rideshare which arrived before Ella had even finished signing the check. He got up, took her by the hand, and led her to the car.

43

They didn't talk much on the ride home, which felt weird and appropriate at the same time. Before Chad came over to their table, Ella was sure that she and Jake were back on track, but now she sensed a bit of iciness between them. He stared out of his car window and she stared out of hers.

Ella took out her phone and resumed the research she'd been doing before Jake met up with her. What were the consequences if she got caught buying an illegal gun in California. Google answers gave her the quick facts that it would be a felony on her record, and $100,000 and/or three years in prison.

Do you really want to deal with that? She asked herself, absentmindedly laying her phone down in her lap.

The logical answer was an easy NO but she couldn't think of a better way to make herself feel safe at home anymore.

"Why are you searching that?" Jake asked, peering over at her phone. She hit the screen lock button to black it out, but it was too late. Should I be honest with him, she asked herself?

"Oh, it's nothing. Don't worry about it," she tried to play it off and he went cold again, looking back out of his window.

The ride was only a few more minutes and they pulled up to one of the mid-city buildings that had been there for decades. Each had their own particular charm and the interior of every apartment had at least one layer of paint on the walls for each tenant who had lived there.

Jake led Ella up three flights of stairs to an apartment at the back corner of the building. Inside it looked exactly as Ella had thought and hoped it would. It was the cleanest bachelor pad she'd ever seen. He had nice dark leather furniture, a trendy bar cart in the corner and a spotless kitchen.

It was always a gamble going to a man's home. Usually, it was how she found out the guy she liked was a total slob or that he never quite transitioned out of his superheroes and hot wheels phase.

"Well, this is home," Jake had an edge to his voice, and Ella sensed this wasn't the way he wanted to spend his night. She could sympathize because it wasn't how she wanted to spend her evening either. This was all Chad's fault.

Ella walked over to the couch while Jake got them a couple of glasses of water, taking the time to pop some ice out of the ice tray before taking it over. "I figure we should have some more water and hydrate before we go for a nightcap," he said, forcing a smile.

"That's a great idea," Ella smiled back, trying to brighten the mood as much as possible.

They made small talk for a little while longer before Jake got up to refill their water glasses. The easy conversation that had flowed between them seemed to have dried up.

"Ok, let's talk about Chad. What the hell happened back there? And why are you researching gun laws?"

Ella had already told him the basics, so it was time to go one level deeper. She sighed, chugged her water, and began.

"Well, remember I told you he was possessive and that's why we broke up? That was all true, but I may have left out some details." Jake's eyes urged her to go on. She could tell he wasn't going to talk until she'd finished. "Ok so there's a lot of stuff in the relationship that I'll skip over for now, but recently Chad has been popping up in my life again. He saw us on our date, he was showing up at the bars I went to. And last week I ran into him while he was moving into my apartment building."

Ella paused, once again taking in Jake's reaction to see if he was as shocked as she felt, but he gave away nothing. "So, I'd planned to stay at Mindy's last week while I sorted out what my options were — spoiler alert, there are none. I'm too broke to live anywhere else without getting a roommate and frankly, I'd rather take my chances in a building with Chad.

"Anyways, it turns out I'd needed a place to stay anyway because the apartment above mine burst their bathroom pipes and they had to redo my apartment. You already know that part, but what you don't know is that it was Chad's apartment. And the workers left my door open all week, so anyone had easy access in and out.

"When I got back, the door was unlocked and there was a pin in it; a lock picking pin. So I asked a friend of mine who knows people if she could help me get a gun because it takes a long time to get them legally in California and who knows what will happen to me before then."

Ella exhaled, not realizing how fast she'd been talking just to get this story out. She'd left out the part about the video but figured she should tell him to complete the picture.

"Wow, ok. That's a lot," Jake said, and she was still unable to read even the slightest inkling of what he was thinking.

Feeling frustrated, Ella grabbed both of their empty water glasses and got up to refill them, adding the rest of the ice and filling the tray with water.

"Pile that creepy video on all of that and, I don't know," Ella shrugged, out of words to describe how overwhelming everything felt.

44

Now it was Jake's turn to get up and make some drinks, but this time he walked over to the bar cart.

"That's a lot to take in," he calmly, grabbing two lowball glasses from the cart and filling them with a finger of whiskey. He sat back down, searching for the right thing to say.

Ella felt that she'd done enough talking for now and sat there waiting for Jake to say whatever was on his mind.

"Ok, well I guess let's start with the obvious. I really don't think you should buy a gun. Especially not an illegal one."

"Why not?" Ella could sense herself getting defensive and tried to mentally tell herself to calm down and hear him out.

"Have you ever shot a gun?"

"No, but I don't see how it could be that hard."

"It's not that it's hard, it's that it's dangerous if you don't know what you're doing. And most people who buy guns thinking the way you are end up getting shot by their own weapon."

She was quiet. He continued.

"Are you prepared to murder someone?"

"What?!" she asked alarmed.

"Are you ready to kill someone? Because that's what a protective gun is there for. To kill."

"I mean, I would rather *not*."

"That's a relief," he tried to lighten the moment a little. It only barely worked.

"Look, I think it's smart for people to protect themselves, but you need to know what you're getting into first. Let alone the legal trouble you'd get into if you actually had to use the gun."

Ella was quiet and sighed. "Yeah, I guess you're right."

"Why don't I take you to the shooting range sometime then you can decide if you want to get one?" he asked.

"Wait, do *you* know how to shoot a gun? Is there one here right now?!" she asked, feeling a little panicked that she was potentially in the room with a deadly weapon, then immediately realizing how stupid that was if she also wanted one with her.

"If you have a gun for protection, you never tell people about it. Otherwise, it becomes a weakness."

"God, this is so stressful," she said, gulping her whiskey down in one drink.

"So, Chad..." Jake started.

"Yeah, Chad," Ella responded.

"What are you going to do about him?"

"I don't know," Ella flopped back on the couch, feeling the many defeats of this week raining down on her. "I honestly do not know. I guess just find a way to live with him in the building? All of my friends think that I'm overreacting about him. They never believed that he's as dangerous as he is."

"For what it's worth, I believe you," Jake said then he leaned over to kiss her. Ella wanted to kiss him back, but now wasn't the time. She was stressed, scared, and the impact of just how drunk she was hit her.

"Sorry, Jake. I'm really sorry but I just don't feel up to anything tonight. Is that ok?"

"Oh, um, yeah sure. I get it." He awkwardly got up, grabbed their glasses and took them to the kitchen, trying to save face. "I'll just get a blanket and a pillow. You can take my bed."

Ella was consistently surprised by how thoughtful he was, even in less-than-ideal situations. "No way! I'm not putting you out. You've done enough. I'll just crash here on the couch and sneak out in the morning."

"Whatever you want to do," he said, and Ella couldn't read if he was angry, annoyed, or just drunk and tired. Even though she was sure she was wrong, she chose to think that he was just tired.

Jake disappeared down the hall and returned a few moments later with a few blankets that smelled like fresh laundry and a pillow. "If you need anything, just come wake me up," he said before he turned out the light and disappeared into his room.

Ella lay there in the dark feeling very drunk, very tired, and very confused. She started to nod off when she thought that she heard a noise from the hallway. It's an unfamiliar building and these are probably normal noises here, she tried to reassure herself.

She couldn't help it though and peeked around at the front door, looking at the sliver of light coming in from under the door. At first it looked like there were two foot-sized shadows there. She blinked, willing herself to see straight, and the shadows were gone.

45

Ella woke up as the blue light of morning started creeping in through the windows. In those first moments, she wasn't sure where she was. Looking around, realizing she was on a couch, it came back to her that she was at Jake's apartment.

It was no small miracle that she didn't feel hungover, just tired thanks to a restless night. She checked her phone. It was 5am and she had 7% battery left. Not wanting to have to wake Jake up to ask for a charger, she opened up the rideshare app, in a hurry to get in a ride before her phone died.

The car was five minutes away, just enough time for her to gather her things and head downstairs. She didn't know Jake's address and hoped that the location her phone showed her at was accurate.

Checking one last time to make sure she hadn't left anything behind, Ella snuck out the front door, making sure to lock the doorknob from the inside before she went. She wondered how many times she'd paid attention to this in the past, or if she was only very recently this concerned with safety.

She walked down to the street just in time to see her car pulling up. She got in and started replaying the night in her mind. She cringed at the thought of their failed kiss, but the regret was short lived. She knew it was a smart decision not to take things any further with Jake for now. She had too much to think about without adding sex into the mix. But her previous experience with men also made her worry that by not sleeping with him, he'd think she was uninterested. Right now, she was willing to take that chance. Besides, Jake seemed like a nice guy, he wouldn't be like the others, right?

In the early morning, the car hit almost all green lights and made it to her apartment in a record 10 minutes. It would usually take at least twice that long at any other time of day.

Grateful that there was no one around, Ella let herself into her apartment, hearing nothing but silence the whole way there. She wasn't sure why, but she hesitated a little as she put her key in the lock and turned it.

But on the other side, everything was exactly as she'd left it. Nothing looked out of place as she hung up her keys, making sure that she locked the door behind her. Sleepiness overwhelmed her, and the last thing she remembered doing before collapsing on her bed was plugging her phone into her charger.

46

Whenever Ella woke up from a nap, she always had a small moment of dread, wondering how many notifications would be on her phone, and if she'd missed anything urgent.

This time, since it was only around noon on a Saturday, there wasn't much she'd missed. A couple of news alerts giving her an update on how many people climate change was going to kill in the next decade. Another showing that her friend had tweeted a meme about cooking vs. going out to eat. Then she had two text messages. One was from Trix.

TRIX: See you tonight! Don't be late...

Ella was not ready to deal with this yet and went to the next one.

JAKE: Hey, it was good seeing you last night. Sorry if this is a little weird, but I think we should slow things down, just be friends for now. We both just have a lot going on. Me and my parents. You and Chad.

Ella could feel the little bit of her heart she'd opened up begging closing back down. She read his second one, bracing for the worst.

JAKE: I'm serious about being friends though. Let me know when you're free and I'll take you to the shooting range. And if you need anything, give me a call and I'll be right over. You're not overreacting.

She softened a little, choosing to believe he was being genuine and not playing games with her or trying to fake break things off.

ELLA: Thanks, Jake. That means a lot. [hugging emoji] And thanks for believing me. Talk soon!

She hit send, not expecting a response, which was good because she didn't get one.

Now to respond to Trix.

ELLA: Sounds good, I'll be there.

Ella hit send knowing that she was only 50% sure she would go, and even less sure that if she did, she'd actually follow through and buy the gun. But she was 100% sure she still felt unsafe and needed to do something about it.

47

Trix hadn't texted Ella again, which made Ella feel like she had no way out now. If Trix had tried to confirm again, Ella knew there was a good chance she'd have tried to chicken out and not meet her friend.

Why does it matter so much that I follow through on this? Ella wondered. Won't he just find another person to sell it to anyway?

She started going down a rabbit hole of stories about people who had their own weapons turned against them during break ins. And stories about people who were otherwise upstanding citizens ending up in prison because of an illegally purchased gun. In almost all of these cases, they were bought for protection.

As the time to meet Trix drew closer, Ella got more and more anxious about the whole situation. She didn't want the gun anymore; she was sure of that. But she also didn't want Trix to be in trouble with these people. She'd warned Ella that she needed to be sure about this, and at the time, Ella had been. But it felt like so much had changed in 24 hours.

She was still scared for her safety and needed a plan, but it wasn't this.

ELLA: Trix, I'm so sorry to do this to you, but I can't go through with this. I changed my mind and don't think I'm ready for that kind of responsibility.

Ella tried to keep it vague to avoid any kind of incrimination should something go wrong later. She figured texting her now was better than standing her up completely. Trix didn't respond, which Ella expected. Under normal circumstances it was only a 50/50 chance Trix would reply anyway. Ella sent one last message.

ELLA: Hope this is ok, and thanks for being a great friend.

It sounded trite, but Ella couldn't think of anything else. She walked into her kitchen and surveyed what alcohol she had left. A cheap bottle of pink wine was in the corner, so she opened it up and poured a glass.

Ella kept checking her phone, but she wasn't sure why. She knew Trix wasn't going to say anything to her. And she knew Jake had had enough of her chaos for now. But she

just felt so lonely. It was like she was willing someone —
anyone — to text her, to remember she existed.

But no one did, and Ella slowly drank herself to sleep.

48

Ella was woken up the next morning by the sound of her phone ringing. It was a Sunday, so it was weird that anyone was calling this early, but something told her to answer it. The screen was flashing an unfamiliar number. Then she remembered it's the number for the place where she interviewed. She sat up fast, immediately triggering a wine headache. But she cleared her throat and tried to sound awake and cheery.

"Hello?" Despite her best efforts, she sounded froggy and hungover.

"H-hello? Is this Ella?"

"Yes it's me. Sorry, I think I've come down with a sore throat. How can I help you?"

"Sorry to call on a Sunday. I'm just calling on behalf of everyone here at Zeitgeist to extend you an offer and see if you'd like to come work with us?"

Ella let out a silent cheer in her room, pumping her fists in the air. "Yes! Yes, that'd be great."

"When can you start?"

"Well, anytime really, but I'd like to give my current job two weeks' notice."

"That's fine. And if they'll let you go earlier, please give us a ring. I'm sending over some documents for your background check. It's just standard procedure to make sure we don't have any serial killers running around the office," the voice on the other end of the phone gave a chuckle, like she loved telling this joke as often as she could. It was clearly not the robot woman from the front desk on the other end of the phone.

Ella chuckled along too, trying not to sound as nervous as she was.

"Ok, sounds good. Send them over and I'll get 'em back to you."

"Thanks, and congratulations again. Oh, and I know this is a Sunday, but don't worry, we only work every *other* Sunday."

"Um, ok. That sounds good," Ella tried to sound enthusiastic, but had clearly not asked the right questions if she didn't know that they semi-regularly worked on Sundays. Maybe it was something they could negotiate later on.

The woman on the other end hung up. Ella sat there, trying to push down the anxiety rising in her. She knew half of it was from drinking the night before, but the other half was the anxiety that came with every new job. The background check.

Ella was about as squeaky clean as a person could be. She'd never been arrested, or sued, or even kicked out of a bar. She'd only had one parking ticket in her whole life and it was because she paid for the wrong parking spot in a lot.

But there was the restraining order, and she was always nervous that an employer would see that and assume she was a person who caused problems. After all, she had to have pretty bad judgement to get into a relationship with someone who she had to get a restraining order against later.

Just assume the best, and see what happens, Ella told herself, trying to channel her inner Creel and will some good vibes into her life.

She got off of the couch and decided to try and get her day started. But something was nagging at her and she wasn't sure exactly what it was. Then she realized.

Trix still hadn't texted her back. Had she met with the guy selling her the gun last night? Had he been upset and hurt her? Ella reminded herself that Trix frequently didn't text back, and everything was probably fine. But she picked up her phone to text her anyway.

ELLA: Hey, just checking to make sure you're ok?

She hit send and waited for Trix to say something back. Nothing. Ella locked her phone and tried to get on with her morning.

The cell phone dinged, indicating there was a new email. Ella checked it and it was the authorization for a background check. At least I can digitally sign this one, so I don't have to print it out, she thought to herself.

Before she could take too much time to think about it, Ella
filled out the paperwork, signed it and hit send.

Everything is going to be fine, Ella tried to convince herself.
You've got a new job. You'll be able to move out soon.
Everything is fine. But something was nagging in the back of
her mind. She couldn't pinpoint what it was.

Her phone rang again. What is going on today? she
wondered to herself. This time the number on the front
made her freeze. It was Chad.

49

Ella didn't answer the call in time, but she hadn't ignored it either. She just stood there, staring at the phone, shocked and confused about why he'd be calling her.

Chad's number was still in her phone precisely for a time like this, so that she wouldn't accidentally answer it if she didn't know whose number it was. She let it ring through to her voicemail again.

Still standing, frozen in place, Ella silently prayed for it not to ring again. Then she had a horrifying idea. What if Chad could hear it ringing from upstairs and knew she was home but not picking up. Maybe that's why he kept calling, because he could hear it ringing below.

It started ringing for a third time, and Ella tapped the button to answer.

"Hello?" she said hastily.

"El! Hi! I'm glad you're up," Chad sounded upbeat, like he'd already been awake for hours.

She didn't respond, so he continued. "Uh, I'm sure you're busy so I'll get to the point. I locked myself out of the building, if you can believe it. Mind coming down to let me in?"

"Um, sure. I guess," she said and hung up. Maybe Chad would know where Trix was, Ella realized. She decided to ask him as soon as she got downstairs.

Ella rushed to the bathroom, unimpressed by the reflection that looked back at her. She was torn between wanting to look a little more presentable or risking him thinking that she cleaned herself up for him. She settled on cleaning off her smudged eyeliner, throwing her hair in a bun, and made her way to let him in.

Chad was staring through the window in the door and waved at her as she turned the corner. He really was handsome, she had to admit to herself. The fact that he hadn't had any other serious girlfriends was a giant red flag though.

She opened the door, and matched his greeting with an unenthusiastic, "Hi."

"Thanks for letting me in. Such a lame move, forgetting my keys," Chad laughed in his easy way.

"Yeah it was," Ella said flatly.

"Well, I guess I'll head upstairs then. Thanks for letting me in." Chad headed up the stairs.

"Wait!" Ella said a little too loudly.

Chad turned around concerned and walked back to her, standing closer than she'd like. "What's up?"

"You haven't heard from Trix, have you?" Ella asked a little sheepishly.

"No, not today. We hung out last night but I decided to leave early. Why did something happen?" He seemed genuinely concerned, but also like he was hiding something. Ella couldn't tell if the concern was for her or Trix, and she secretly chided herself for hoping the concern was for her. She was also wondering what he could be hiding, or if she was just imagining the reaction from him.

"Probably not. We just got into a little fight. Well, I think it was a fight, and she hasn't responded to my texts. I just wanted to make sure she's ok." She told him more than she'd meant to, opening up a vulnerable crack that she was hoping he wouldn't notice. But of course he did.

Chad tried to take her hands, in a reassuring way, but Ella pulled them back from him. He sighed. "Look, El. Sometimes you have a habit of making things a bigger deal than they are. I'm sure Trix is fine. You know she keeps weird hours. She's probably just sleeping."

"Yeah, you're probably right. Not about me overreacting though," she said, finding some anger inside herself. "I only let you in because I was on my way out anyway. Don't forget your key again."

"Um, don't you want to put on some shoes first?"

Ella looked down and realized she was wearing fuzzy slippers. She tried to act confident. "No. This is the new style. Everyone is wearing these out."

"Huh. I haven't seen them before. Ok, well, if you ever lock yourself out, I owe you one."

"No thanks," she said before shutting the front door to the building behind her.

As Ella started to walk around the block, her first thought was, I'm definitely going to need some new slippers after this.

50

Ella walked around the block once, positive that she looked like someone who was doing the walk of shame or who was homeless.

Take this time to make your plan for the day, she thought to herself, willing her brain to think about anything besides the flurry of worries that were threatening to take over her mind. There were a ton of things she could do, but the thing that kept nagging at her was Trix. And why did Chad look so disheveled?

There was the possibility he'd forgotten his keys on purpose so that he had a reason to call her, but that was risky, assuming she might not have been home, or might have put her phone on silent.

She resented that he said she sometimes overreacted, though. Why did so many people say this to her? The worst-case scenario didn't always happen, of course, but that's not to say it couldn't, and why not be mentally prepared for that?

Ella rounded the final corner on her block, ready to go back inside and toss her slippers that were now wet with dew from the grass she had to step on to avoid a few couples who were taking up the sidewalk. Walking inside, she decided the next thing she'd do was to drive by Trix's house. She'd rather her friend be annoyed with Ella for coming over than find out she was dying on her floor or something and no one had done anything.

Wow, yeah ok, maybe I am overreacting, she thought as she pushed away the vision of Trix lying dead on her floor, murdered by Chad or the person who was supposed to give her the gun. But I'll think about this all day if I don't go now, Ella resolved to herself.

So, she left her building and headed out to check on Trix.

51

Ella was almost to Trix's apartment when her phone chimed with a text message.

TRIX: All good over here.

A sigh of relief flowed through Ella's entire body. But since she was almost there, she figured she'd still swing by and make sure there were no cop cars outside or anything. There was always the chance Chad had taken Trix's phone or something and he was really the one texting Ella.

She pulled up outside of the apartment. Even though Trix could probably have afforded a house, or something much better than the studio she lived in, she chose to stay and save money. The building wasn't bad or anything, it was just like every other apartment built in LA during the 1970s. Retro, boxy, and a name on the outside announcing to everyone it was The Rosebud. There were no cops outside and everything looked normal. Ella breathed a sigh of relief.

Knowing she seriously needed to chill out, Ella decided to head home and do something constructive with her day. But when she got back, she felt exhausted from the adrenaline that had been rushing through her all morning. Whenever she was anxious for a long time, she realized that she was absolutely spent once her nervous system returned to normal.

Ella parked her car down the block from her building — the first open spot she could find — and started looking around for Chad, certain he was lurking somewhere. She made it safely up to her apartment, took one look at her couch and plopped down on it, mentally and emotionally exhausted.

Ella turned on the TV more out of habit than actually wanting to watch anything, but since it was on, she had to choose something. After scrolling, she settled on the Golden Girls. With the sounds of Dorothy, Blanch, Rose, and Sofia droning on in the background, Ella fell into a deep sleep.

It was shaping up to be a great midday nap when she was jolted awake by a loud knocking at the door. At first Ella thought it was part of her dream, but then it didn't stop. It pulled her out of her deep comfortable sleep, and she realized what was happening. Someone was knocking at her door. They were knocking hard. But she wasn't expecting anyone.

Every woman knows that you don't answer the door if you aren't expecting anyone. She had no plans to open it but was nonetheless curious about who it was.

The knocking stopped for a few moments, and Ella thought maybe the person was gone. Maybe they'd realized they'd been at the wrong apartment.

She walked closer to the door, attempting to look out of the peephole without her floor creaking when a loud KNOCK KNOCK KNOCK rattled the door.

52

Startled, Ella jumped back, letting out a small yelp. She clasped her hand over her mouth, but just as she did, the knocking abruptly stopped, indicating the person on the other side had heard her.

Even though she was feeling rattled, Ella put her eye to the peephole, trying to get a glance at who was on the other side.

No one was there.

Should I open the door and check? she wondered to herself.

On one hand she knew someone could be waiting on the side of the door, just out of eyesight from her peephole. On the other, she knew it would bother her if she didn't at least take a peek to see who was out there.

She took a deep breath, and opened her door a crack, looking to see if anyone was out there or if she could hear any motion. Nothing. Not even a footstep. She opened the door a little wider so she could look up and down the hall. It was empty.

Closing her door, Ella went back to her couch and lied down, trying to will herself back into the sleep she'd been jolted out of. It was no use. Just then Ella's phone chimed.

MINDY: Hey El! Sorry for the short notice but I'm having a housewarming party next Saturday. Think you can make it?
ELLA: Sure! Did you just decide to have it?
MINDY: No, but since you've already been here we didn't think you'd want to come. Then I realized it might be good networking for you!

Ella guessed at what the real story was. Mindy had probably wanted to invite her but Creel said no. Then Mindy came up with a reason and voila, Ella was invited.

ELLA: Good idea. I'll be there.
MINDY: Great! See you then.

Part of Ella wished that Mindy had asked how she was doing, but that was expecting too much of Mindy. Ella knew that after having been friends for so long.

53

The next day, Ella got to work, knowing she had to tackle the awkward task of putting in her two weeks' notice at a place where she'd just finally gotten the hang of the things. But it'll be worth it, she told herself.

First, she'd break the news to Zora. It would be weird not to. She went up to her desk, where she was thankful to find Zora sitting alone, no Jake. Maybe some things would go right for her today after all.

"Hey Zora!" she said cheerfully. A little too cheerful.

Zora turned toward her, wearing a clearly hungover grimace. "Do you mind taking it down a notch? My head is throbbing."

"Oh sure! Sorry. What happened to you?" Ella always felt a little left out when her friends did things without her, but she knew that was needy, so she'd never tell them.

"I was watching the football game at the bar near me. I guess I had a few too many."

"It happens. Hey, sorry to do this but I have something important to tell you." Ella wasn't sure but she thought Zora may have rolled her eyes a little at this.

"Sure, go ahead."

"Well, remember that place I interviewed at?"

Zora perked up. "Yeah?"

"I got the job." Ella was excited but tried to hold it back until she could read Zora's reaction. To Ella's relief, Zora seemed genuinely happy for her. She grabbed Ella's hands.

"That's great! When do you start?"

"In two weeks. I've gotta put in my notice today."

"Well, I'm bummed I don't get to work with you for longer, but I'd be lying if I said I thought you were going to stay here for a long time."

Ella felt so happy to have Zora's support, especially about a big decision like this. "Well, I'm off to type up my resignation."

"Oh, you didn't tell them yet?"

"No, I wanted to tell you first."

"That was thoughtful." Zora smiled at Ella, then got up from her chair. "C'mon, I'll walk down there with you. I need to get more coffee."

54

Ella walked to the kitchen with Zora, grabbed a coffee and headed to her desk. She wasn't too surprised to see that her boss was already there but a little disheartened, nonetheless. She'd hoped she'd at least have a few moments to herself before she had to launch into her resignation. But she decided to rip the Band-Aid off.

"Hi, Janet!" Dammit, too cheerful again, Ella thought to herself.

"Hey Ella," Janet said, barely looking over at her.

Ella sat down and tried to seem nonchalant, but felt awkward, like she was carrying her resignation on the outside of her body. "Do you have a second?"

Janet turned to Ella, curiously. "Yeah, sure. What's up?"

"Well, I hate to do this but, I'm turning in my two weeks."

Janet looked genuinely surprised, which made Ella feel a little better since it meant that Janet wasn't relieved, she was leaving.

"That's too bad," Janet said. "You were just getting into a rhythm."

"I know. I feel awful leaving so soon, but an opportunity came up that I couldn't pass on."

"I understand. Hey, this place isn't for everyone. Don't worry about it. Actually, I think we've got a junior social media person who could step in."

"Oh!" Ella said. Maybe she'd misread Janet after all. It hadn't even been a full 60 seconds and she'd already been replaced. "Oh, that's great. I wouldn't want you to lose time training another person."

"Me neither," Janet said matter-of-factly. "I'll talk to her manager and see if you can start training her today.

"That's great," Ella said.

The junior person didn't come over that day, but Ella spent the day making onboarding documents for her anyway, so any transition, whether it was this person or not, would be a smooth one.

Overall, she felt good about how the day had gone. Zora and Janet both took the news well, and that's the best Ella could have hoped for.

She parked at her apartment, walked inside, and up the stairs to her door. There was something orange at her doorstep.

Ella felt like she both simultaneously froze and yet floated toward her door. She stared down at the envelope, which had her name written on it in big, blocky Sharpie-drawn letters. ELLA.

55

She didn't want to pick it up, but what other choice did she have? I'll open it here in the hallway, that way if it's something dangerous I can get help, she thought to herself, acknowledging that seemed like an overcautious reaction. But there was something comforting about knowing she was closer to other people out here than in her apartment. This envelope was slim, and she wondered if there was anything in it at all.

Pinching the brass clasps together to open the envelope, Ella unfolded the flap. There was something inside. It was a white sheet of paper. She pulled it out, confused about what she was seeing. Then she turned the paper over.

It was a still frame of her sleeping, taken from the anonymous video she'd been sent.

Ella held the paper in her hand, staring in disbelief. She now felt the need to get inside her apartment as fast as possible.

Once inside her apartment, Ella dropped the picture and the envelope on the ground and went directly to the cabinet for a bottle of wine. She didn't even care which one, she just pulled a bottle, opened it, and took a swig without bothering to use a glass.

She stared at the picture lying on her floor, taunting her, and decided to come up with a plan. It was so clear now that Chad was behind this. Her life had been fine until she'd seen him in the bar a few weeks ago. Since then, he'd found her at every turn, and that's when she'd received the unsettling video. But what she was determined *not* to do was to let Chad, or anyone get the best of her. Not anymore.

Grabbing her wine bottle, Ella went to her couch, pulled out her computer, and started looking up security cameras. There were lots on the market at about every price point possible. She decided she could only afford the cheapest one, $45.99, with a $10 monthly service fee. I'll just have to cut back on my wine budget, she told herself as she took a swig from the bottle.

She finished purchasing the camera, which promised to be at her apartment in a week. That seemed like a long way away, but Ella figured if she had lasted this long without one, she could handle another week.

The envelope and photo were still lying on the ground by the door. Feeling liquid courage running through her, Ella walked over, picked them up and stuffed them in the trash.

56

The next day at work, Ella met the woman who would be taking her job. Her name was Hayley. She was young, blonde, and looked like she might even be an influencer herself. Then again, everyone thought they were influencers in LA, Ella thought.

Apparently, Hayley had managed to talk her way into getting promoted to Ella's job, not just taking over until they could find someone else. Ella had heard this about this happening, but it was usually called something like "advocating for yourself." Ella had always been too scared to do that, assuming she'd negotiate herself out of a job instead of into one.

Over the following days, Ella taught Hayley everything she'd need to know, and they worked side-by-side doing their work. By Thursday, Ella barely needed to do anything. Hayley had picked up the job very quickly, which left Ella wondering if she might even be able to leave the job a week earlier and use her vacation pay for a break in-between jobs.

As she was mulling this over, her phone rang. It was her new job calling. A wave of panic rose in Ella's chest as she wondered why in the world they'd be calling her. She walked out of the building to take the call.

"Hello?"

"Hi, Ella?"

"Yes?" Was something wrong with her background check? Had they found something she didn't even know was on there? Calm down. They'll tell you why they're calling if you just calm down, her internal monologue said.

"Hi, this is Angelica at Zeitgeist."

"Oh, yes. How can I help you?"

"I hate to have to tell you this, but we can no longer offer you the position here."

Ella felt the ground fall from beneath her. "Um, I'm sorry. What do you mean?"

"I know this isn't what you'd hoped to hear."

It most certainly was not!

The voice on the other end continued. "Unfortunately, the company has decided to downsize the department you were getting hired into."

"I see," Ella was numb.

"This has nothing to do with you. You're a great candidate and we are confident that you'll find a job somewhere else."

Ella said nothing on the other end.

"Ella? Are you there?"

"Yeah, yeah I'm here. Sorry. Ok well, thanks for the call," Ella said, and hung up, unsure if the woman was still talking or not, but there was nothing she could say that would put Ella at ease.

She now had no job at all and needed to try and beg her way back into her current job which had already been filled.

57

Ella was trying desperately not to hyperventilate in the parking lot. She was exactly where she'd been a month ago. Jobless with no prospects and wondering what she'd do next. Humbling herself, Ella walked back into the building.

Janet was sitting next to Hayley, looking like they'd been working together for months. I should have done a worse job training her, Ella thought to herself. She took a deep breath, stood up straight, and walked over to them. She knelt down next to Janet, on the opposite side from Hayley.

"Hey, Janet. Do you have a minute to talk?" Ella said, trying to sound as chill as possible.

"Um, yeah, sure," Janet said in a way that meant she in fact did not have a minute to talk. But she only turned her chair towards Ella, she didn't get up.

Ella stood, motioning to a corner of the room. "Oh, actually do you mind if we talk over there?"

"Um, sure. Ok." Janet stood and reluctantly walked to the corner, following Ella's lead, clearly annoyed that she was being asked to do this.

Once they were out of earshot of anyone, Ella began explaining. "So, this is incredibly awkward for me, but I just got a call from the company I was going to work for, and they just downsized the department I was going into."

Ella paused, and she was glad she did because Janet's entire expression changed to a sympathetic one. "Oh, Ella. That's awful. I'm sorry to hear that," Janet said, and Ella thought for a moment that Janet might even try to hug her.

"It's ok. Not a big deal. I just need to ask — and I hate to do this. You have no idea how much I hate to do this — but I have to ask if I can have my job back here?"

"I'm so sorry, but that's not possible. Hayley has already signed her promotion papers. That ship has sailed," Janet said.

Ella was crestfallen. "No, yeah, yeah, of course. Of course! Yeah, I get it. But you can't blame a girl for trying," she tried to laugh it off, as though she wasn't screaming inside.

They were quiet, standing there together for long enough that it became awkward. Janet finally gave in and hugged Ella, looking like she wasn't sure what else to do to end the sad tension. It was one of those far-away hugs, where the only part of her body that actually touched Ella was Janet's hands on Ella's back. While Ella was happy to get a drip of sympathy from anyone, the hug somehow made the moment worse.

Ella returned the gesture just as Janet gave Ella a quick double pat on the back, indicating the hug was over.

"Ok well, do you mind if I take the rest of the day off and deal with this?" Ella asked.

"Yes of course. Take tomorrow too if you need it."

"Thanks, but at this point I'd rather cash in the vacation pay. Something tells me I might need it," Ella laughed nervously. She was sure it sounded forced, but she didn't care anymore.

Ella turned to leave, then Janet called her back. "Ella?"

Whirling around, Ella wondered if Janet had changed her mind. Maybe she'd figured out a way to keep her on after all! "Don't you want to get your purse?" Janet asked.

"Oh. Right, yes of course. Thank you," Ella said, still trying to somehow sound calm and collected

She walked to her desk, grabbed her bag, and headed out of the office.

58

Once she was driving home, Ella wondered if she should have gone upstairs and told Zora before leaving. Maybe she'd have some advice or know of other positions in the company. Then again, Ella knew she'd still leave the moment she was given a chance and she couldn't do that twice to Zora.

The drive home seemed to take only seconds, with Ella's mind racing through what she was going to do now. She would hit the job boards that had become like a second online home to her now. But other than that, she realized she'd exhausted most of her options during her initial job search.

Hurrying up to her apartment, Ella resisted the urge to pour herself a drink. Instead, she sat down on her couch and opened up their group chat.

ELLA: Bad news. I don't have a job.
ZORA: Um... what?

Ella hadn't planned on Zora responding that quick. Maybe it was a mistake to tell the group before telling her first. Then again, might as well get it over with. She didn't want to have to go through this twice.

ELLA: The new job called me back and said they were eliminating the department that was hiring me, and they already promoted someone into my current job... so I'm SOL.
LULU: Yikes. Tough luck.
MINDY: Maybe you'll meet someone you can work with at my housewarming this weekend!
ELLA: Yeah *fingers crossed*
TRIX: You can always come work with me.
ELLA: Who knows, maybe it'll come down to that.
TRIX: Don't sound too excited.
LULU: Omg as if you'd do that. Can you even dance?

Ella tried to remember a time when she wasn't annoyed with Lulu, but nothing came to mind. She was forever bothered by her transparent efforts to put everyone down so Mindy would want to only hang out with her.

ZORA: That sucks, El.
ELLA: Why is all of this happening to me?

She was hoping for a stronger show of sympathy from them. She knew she'd had her share of drama lately, but that was life. Were they getting tired of her? Could friends do that? Just get tired of each other?

MINDY: Go home, pour yourself a glass of vino and chill. You'll find something. Stay positive!

Ella didn't respond. She was so sick of Mindy's insistence that being positive changed everything. Sometimes life just didn't go your way and that was that.

59

The next few days flew by in a haze for Ella. She spent every moment looking for jobs, applying for them, trying to bid for freelance work, anything that could help her make ends meet until she found something else.

Before she knew it, Saturday rolled around and it was time to get ready for Mindy's party. Finding an outfit was tricky because Ella wanted to look attractive, but in a way that would make people take her seriously. In the end, she chose a black shift dress that was short enough to be fun, but not too short.

A rideshare wasn't in her current budget, but Ella knew a DUI wasn't in her budget either, so she tapped a few buttons and got a car that was minutes away.

In her cooped up, anxiety-fueled application frenzy that week, Ella hadn't thought about Chad or the prospect of running into him until now. She hadn't even left her apartment at all except for one trip to the store to grab some soup and other cheap things she could eat to tide her over until Saturday.

Ella hadn't realized it until she stepped in the car, but there was actually a lot of pressure to make a job connection with someone tonight. She looked over her outfit again and was pleased with the choice.

The ride to Mindy's seemed to fly by. Ella's mind was numb from the stress of job hunting and wondering if she'd be able to keep her apartment or if she'd have to ask one of her friends if she could crash on her couch.

The car arrived, breaking Ella's stream of consciousness. She thanked the driver and got out.

Mindy's house looked even more stunning and somehow also quaint in the moonlight. Like it was the only little bungalow in the world. Ella could hear the hum of people inside as she walked toward the door where a waiter was standing, holding a tray of champagne. She took one glass, downed it, then placed the empty flute back on the tray before grabbing another. With a little "cheers" gesture to the waiter, she walked in.

A quick survey of the living room proved that she didn't know a soul who was in there. Ella started circling the outside of the living room, trying to get a glimpse of Mindy, or any friendly face really, but had no luck.

That's when she heard the shrill voice, she constantly forgot existed: Lulu.

"Ella!" Lulu screeched, sounding overly excited.

"Lulu! Hi," Ella said, reaching out to give Lulu what Ella now called "a Janet hug.".

"I didn't know we'd be seeing you here," Lulu chirped.

"Well, here I am."

"Here you are!"

Ella could sense an awkward silence settling on them, so she asked, "Hey, have you seen Mindy anywhere?"

"She's still getting ready in her room. I'm sure she'll be out soon. She asked me to help welcome the guests until she got here."

"Oh, ok great. Well, hiiii!" Ella didn't know why she disliked Lulu so much. Yeah, she was annoying but something about her seemed deceptive and Ella never found it easy to be around someone she distrusted.

"Sorry about losing your job," Lulu said, with what looked like a genuine look of sympathy.

"Oh thanks. I guess that's just the way sometimes."

"Isn't it just," Lulu smiled, the content of the conversation not matching the broad, sparkling smile Lulu was wearing, as if she actually relished that Ella was out of a job again. Then her smile broke as something behind Ella caught her eye. She waved to someone she couldn't see. "Sorry, Ella, but I've got to go greet the guests. Mindy will be out soon."

"Great, thanks," Ella said, but Lulu had already pushed by her and was hugging the newly arriving guests.

Then she heard a deep voice next to her. "Having fun yet?" Ella turned around to see a man standing next to her. He was tall, wearing the usual LA uniform of $100 jeans, a plain white tee, and a black blazer. He seemed a little older, with salt and pepper hair, but a full head of it. Ella was clearly caught off guard because he said, "Sorry, I didn't mean to startle you."

"Oh, oh no it's fine," she tried to save herself from looking like a fool and laughing it off. "I just didn't know anyone was standing so close to me."

"I saw you walk in, and once Lulu was the first person you talked to, well, I figured you knew as few people here as I do."

His words put Ella at ease. If this handsome man could feel out of place here, then she shouldn't feel so bad. She flashed what she hoped was a charming smile and extended her hand. "Hi, I'm Ella."

He shook her hand, firm but not too firm like he was trying to show off his strength. "Spencer."

"So, what brings you to this soiree, Ella?"

Ella always found herself a little uncomfortable around people who were good at making small talk. But she tried to remind herself he could be a potential employer, and to treat this as a pre-interview. That proved instantly difficult because he was just so striking. "Mindy has been my friend since we were kids," she finally sputtered out.

"Is that right? That's a rare thing to find these days."

"What is?"

"People who were childhood friends rarely stay that way, let alone end up living in the same city."

"Oh, right. Yes. Well..." she'd already run out of things to say. Then she remembered... "What about you? What brings you here?"

"I worked with Mindy at her last job."

"And what did you do there?"

He chuckled in a way that made Ella wish she hadn't asked the question. "I own the company."

"I see..." Now she had no idea what to say and raised her glass instead. "Well, cheers to that, huh?"

He laughed easily and clinked his glass to hers. They both took a sip and Ella was glad for the quick moment to think.

"What kind of business do you own?"

He looked surprised. "You mean Mindy didn't talk about it? I'm hurt." He added the last part sarcastically.

Ella held back the embarrassment that threatened to flush her cheeks. "Yeah! No, yeah for sure she did. I just mean, I want to hear it from the man himself. What's your elevator pitch?" Did she save herself, she wondered?

"It's just a PR company. Nothing too important." He was being humble and it showed.

"I'm sure it's more than that."

He winked and took another sip of his champagne. Ella followed his lead and sipped her own. "So, what do you do, Ella?"

Here it was. The question she was dreading. "I'm actually between jobs right now."

"Ahh, I see. What is it you used to do?"

"Well, I was a Social Media Manager. Then I quit because I got a job offer to be a Content Strategist, but before I could start, they downsized the department, and my other job had already been filled by someone internally. So, here I am," Ella said, lifting her hands and shrugging.

"Here you are," Spencer said, looking at her inquisitively. Ella couldn't figure out if this was a good or bad thing. He gestured to their glasses. "You know what? I don't really like champagne."

"Me neither."

"What do you say we finish these off and go find where Mindy keeps the good stuff. I'm sure her childhood friend has an idea."

"I know exactly where the good stuff is," Ella smiled, wondering how it was suddenly so easy to talk to him. Must be the champagne, she thought.

"And maybe we can talk about if there's a spot for you at my company. We're always looking for someone eager to come aboard, and it sounds like you have a lot of experience."

"I'll drink to that!" She blurted out a bit too enthusiastically.

60

By the time Zora got to the party, Ella was full blown drunk. She wasn't stumbling around yet, but she was loud and completely absorbed in talking with Spencer. In fact, Ella had forgotten Zora was even coming and stopped keeping an eye out for her. She only remembered when Zora found her and Spencer sitting in the backyard with a bottle sitting next to them.

"Zora!" Ella exclaimed. "Zora, come sit down. Grab a glass and come sit."

"Ok, I just want to say hi to Mindy. Have you seen her?"

Ella realized that she'd been so absorbed in her conversation with Spencer that she hadn't even thought to go find Mindy. Clearly Spencer hadn't either. "No, I couldn't find her earlier, and I've been out here with Spencer ever since."

Zora extended her hand to Spencer. "Hi, I'm Zora."

"Another childhood friend?" he asked.

"No, just a regular one," she returned. "I'll be back."

Ella turned back to Spencer, but Zora's appearance had made her see that she was much drunker than just buzzed now. She looked down at her cup which was near empty.

"Another?" he asked, picking up the bottle to pour her some more.

Everything in her wanted another drink. "No thanks. I'm good for now," she set down her glass as she said it, creating distance between herself and the liquid that was left in it.

"A lightweight, huh?" he laughed, sitting back in his own seat and taking a drink from his own lowball.

"Just pacing myself. But where were we? I think you were about to offer me a job," she laughed knowing that was likely not what he was going to do, but where was the harm in asking?

"That's right. I was. I was about to tell you that we can offer you the Social Media Specialist position starting at $80,000/year with incentive-based bonuses, and health benefits, of course. What do you say?"

Ella was dumbfounded. She really didn't think she was going to get an offer, let alone such a specific and generous one. "Um, wow." was all she could blurt out.

Spencer was sitting back with a satisfied smile on his face, crunching a piece of ice between his teeth he'd fished out during his last sip. "So, is that a yes?"

Ella picked up her glass with what little liquid was remaining. "To new jobs," she said, lifting her glass and clinking his. She downed what was left of her drink as Zora walked up, holding her own glass of what looked like vodka soda.

"Looks like I've just missed something," she said curiously.

"You have," Spencer confidently answered. "Ella, would you like to tell her?"

"Spencer has offered me a job," Ella said a little sheepishly.

"Wow! That's- that's great!" Zora said, with a rare moment of genuine excitement, which made Ella feel more excited too.

They sat there, chatting and drinking for a while, Ella wasn't sure how long. She just knew that by the time Mindy spotted them in the back, they all appeared to have known each other for ages.

"I see I'm missing quite the good time over here," Mindy said, obviously salty none of them except Zora had come to find her. She looked gorgeous as always, but when someone looked like her, it was hard to discern one glamorous moment from the next. They all overlapped.

Spencer set down his drink and got up, giving her the obligatory two-cheek air kiss. "Mindy! You never told me you had such charming friends!"

"I didn't know I did!" Mindy said coolly, then quickly added, "Kidding!" with a laugh that was a bit too hard. "Yes, Ella and I go way back. And Zora is about as consistent of a person as you can find.

"Consistent? What a compliment," Zora added a bit sarcastically.

"Well, you know what I mean," Mindy said.

"It's good to know you and Ella have similar roots because I've offered her your old job," Spencer beamed.

Ella was taken aback but tried to hide it. She hadn't realized this was Mindy's job she was backfilling. But Mindy couldn't have been happier. She was so excited it seemed a little fake, Ella thought. "That's WONDERFUL news!! See, Ella? I told you if you came here you'd be able to find a job. You made quick work of it, too. Oh, that makes me so happy!" Mindy gushed.

"Thanks, Min," Ella said, warmed by how genuinely thrilled her most critical friend was for her.

"Well, I've got to circulate, but I see you're all doing fine over here. Just make sure you don't talk shop all night, ok?" she laughed, lifting her champagne flute in salute to them before leaving.

And after that, the rest of the night went to shit for Ella.

61

Ella got a little carried away the rest of the night, feeling a wave of relief at not having to continue her job hunt. She also felt overwhelming gratitude for Mindy inviting her here, even though Ella was sure it caused a fight with Creel. She even started to rethink Mindy's directives to always stay positive. Maybe it worked after all.

Towards the end of the party, it was clear Ella had drunk too much. Zora called her a car and was going to send her home alone until Ella freaked out, realizing that this would mean she would have to get home and hope Chad wouldn't see her stumbling in, and take advantage of the situation.

"Look, you're not as drunk as you think," Zora said, trying to build Ella's confidence.

"And you're not as worried about me as you should be!" Ella tried not to yell but she was pretty sure it came out that way.

Zora looked around, sighed heavily, and closed Ella's door. Then she walked around to the other side and got in.

Feeling relieved for the second time that night, Ella rested her head on Zora's shoulder and closed her eyes. By the time she opened them again they were in front of her apartment.

That quick nap had done wonders for Ella, and she was easily able to get out of the car, with Zora next to her. They quietly walked up the stairs and Ella did her best to noiselessly unlock her locks but on the last one, she dropped her keys. They crashed to the floor with a loud jangle. Panicked, she picked them up and fumbled to get the lock open. She rushed in and pulled Zora in after her.

"Think you have enough locks?" Zora asked, half joking and half worried for her friend's sanity.

"No actually. I'm not sure at all. But it'll do until my security cameras get here," Ella responded.

"Ok, well you're inside safe. Why don't you get changed and I'll bring you some water."

Ella followed directions and walked into her room, slipping off her dress and pulling on some sweats. She caught her reflection in the mirror, and even though she was still drunk, what she saw was disheveled enough that she had to take a few moments to clean herself up before she subjected Zora to seeing herself like this again.

She came back out to the living room and Zora was standing there, holding a glass of water, and looking curiously at Ella's door locks.

"You really are scared of him, huh?"

Ella felt embarrassed as she took the water and sat down on the couch. "Sometimes. Most of the time, I can convince myself he's harmless. Then I'll hear him moving around upstairs or I'll catch a glimpse of him walking around, and I get that fear all over again."

"I guess that's only natural. But you do know he's probably moved on by now, right? People change. They get their hearts broken and they move on."

"You're probably right. Don't you think it's so weird he moved into my building though?"

"Yeah, I think that's the weirdest, creepiest part of this whole thing," Zora was honest and Ella was thankful for it.

"But that doesn't mean he's trying to do anything bad. You live in an up-and-coming part of town and have rent control. Lots of people would want to live here."

"And what about him moving *right above me*?"

"Yup. That's totally weird too. It's a weird coincidence though. He couldn't have planned that. Someone moved out and he moved in."

"I guess you're right," Ella said, trying to lean into the logic Zora was offering her. She got up and hugged her friend. "Thanks, I appreciate you coming home with me."

"No problem," Zora walked towards the door. "Don't forget to lock these after me, ok?"

Ella gave a sheepish laugh.

Zora walked into the hall and heard the locks start turning behind her. She laughed to herself and glanced up at the stairs leading to the floor Chad lived on.

62

The sound of ringing woke Ella up. At first, she thought it was in her head, as she started to feel the massive headache she had taking hold of her. Then she realized it was her phone ringing. She fumbled for it, finally finding it, but she didn't recognize the number.

A flood of panic came over her as she tried to decide whether to answer it or not. The decision was made for her when it finally got sent over to her voicemail. She wondered who it could be, running over the list of people she could think of. It was a Sunday morning, and most of her friends had been at the party last night so she was sure it wasn't any of them. In the back of her mind, she worried it was the mysterious video sender, but she didn't let herself think too long about that.

The voicemail icon popped up and she tapped it, holding her breath to see what voice would float through the other end.

"This message is for Ella. I'm calling on behalf of Spencer to give you the details of starting your new job tomorrow," the female matter-of-fact voice explained. Tomorrow seemed so fast to start, but then again, she needed the money, so it was probably best. "You'll come to 777 Highland at 8am. There is underground parking. We'll validate your ticket. Give the receptionist your name and you'll be walked to your workstation. Spencer will meet you there. Please call back at the number I called you from if you have any questions. See you tomorrow and welcome to the team."

Ella saved the message, knowing she'd need to write down the details later. Then she flopped back in her bed feeling grateful for how this had worked out. She'd doubted Mindy when she told Ella to go there to network, but it all turned out for the best.

Then the dread started setting in. PTSD from so many jobs won and lost, Ella started to plan for what happened if this didn't work out. Even though she'd start tomorrow, they'd likely have to go through all of the background and credit checks, wouldn't they? What if they decided she was too credit-poor to work for them? She could barely afford to eat lunch out with who she hoped would be her new office friends.

Don't think like that, she chastised herself. Think positively.

But no matter how hard she tried, the dread set in again. Now that she was firmly awake, Ella got up to make herself some coffee and find something to eat to calm her hangover. She found everything she needed to make a breakfast burrito in her fridge and it felt like nothing short of a miracle.

After she'd made herself some food, she grabbed her laptop and settled in on her couch to start looking into applying for unemployment benefits. She'd feel better knowing she had a Plan B to fall back on this time.

Her phone chimed, letting her know she had a text, but between her burrito, which had turned out to be quite messy, and the focus she needed to fill out these forms, she ignored it for now. Then it buzzed two more times. Ella hastily ate the rest of her burrito, downed her cup of coffee, and went to the kitchen to wash off the remnants of hot sauce and pour another cup.

She plopped back on the couch and unlocked her phone, staring at the screen for only a moment before dropping it on the ground.

The three messages were from Chad.

63

Ella sat straight up, frozen and suddenly wide awake. Chad. She hesitated to click on the messages, not really sure if she wanted to know what he had to say, but also certain that if she didn't look, her anxiety would get the best of her.

She tapped on them.

CHAD: Hey, I'm sorry to bother you, but can you talk?
CHAD: I think it's over with Trix, and I know she thought it was casual, but I'm taking it pretty hard.
CHAD: If you don't want to talk, I understand.

What the hell, Ella thought to herself. Out of all of the people he could text, why did he choose her? Then she remembered Chad never really had many friends. He just obsessed about her most of the time they were together.

Weighing her next move, Ella heard his footsteps above her. They were light, not like he was stomping, but more like slow pacing. She got up and stared at the phone, then hit reply.

ELLA: Um, sure? Do you want to just call me?

Ella wasn't sure why she said yes, especially when she didn't trust him. She heard the footsteps above her stop, then her phone dinged.

CHAD: I need to see a friendly face.

She sighed. There was no way she was going to be alone with him, but something in her still had a softness for him. Despite the trauma, drama, and overall creepiness, she knew at his core he was a broken person like everyone else.

ELLA: How about we go on a walk around the block then?

The reply was fast.

CHAD: Sure! Thanks, I appreciate it.

Ella threw on her least flattering clothes, trying to make sure she looked unattractive so he wouldn't get any ideas. Then she walked out of her apartment, down the steps, and there he was waiting in the lobby. He smiled a sad smile. "Thanks again. I know it's early. I'm just having a hard time."

"Ok, well, go ahead and tell me about it," Ella wanted to seem cold and uninterested, maybe make him think that calling her had been a mistake and he wouldn't do it again.

They left the lobby and started walking. It was already warm and sunny out. People were busy heading to their fitness classes or brunch or whatever people did this early on a Sunday.

"Well, Trix is great. You know that already. She's so vibrant, and she's so smart. She warned me not to get attached at the beginning, so I didn't. I tried really hard. I didn't text her or see her unless she initiated."

"What happened?" Ella asked, remembering Trix telling her it wasn't serious between them.

"That's the thing. *She* called *me* and told me she wanted to break up because she was starting to have feelings for me. Apparently by acting exactly the way she'd asked me to, I'd become what she was looking for in someone."

Ella thought this sounded a little too emotional for Trix to do something like that, but Trix was also about as unpredictable as a person could be. She found herself believing Chad, and even though she tried not to, she felt bad for the guy.

"Ok, so what do you want me to do?" she asked a little more harshly than she meant to, but maybe that was for the best.

"I don't know. When I first thought about texting you to talk, I thought that I really did just need to get this off my chest. But now, I'm wondering if maybe you could put a good word in for me with Trix?"

"I don't know. I don't like getting involved in other people's business. And that would sound pretty rich coming from me, the person who has been telling her not to date you in the first place," as soon as she said that last part, Ella wished she could pull back the words.

Chad gave a small gasp, "You— you did? Why would you do that?"

Now it was time to be honest. "Because you were a bad boyfriend, Chad. People don't get restraining orders for good boyfriends, do they?" She watched his face carefully to see how her words had affected him. Both of them had subconsciously sped up their paces.

"Wow, I thought you were just going through something. I didn't know you genuinely thought I was a bad boyfriend."

"You were following me around!" Ella said a little too loudly, drawing some looks from passersby. She quieted herself. "That's why I had to get the restraining order because you wouldn't stop following me."

"Wait, you thought I was *stalking* you? Ella, I just wanted to make sure you were safe. Anyone who knows you knows that you can get a little careless when you drink. And even if we weren't together anymore, I still cared about you and wanted to make sure you weren't getting taken advantage of."

Ella registered that he'd said, "cared." Did he truly not care about her anymore? Had he really been just trying to make sure she was safe?

"What about you moving into my same building and dating my friend?"

"You have one of the best, most affordable buildings in the city and I'm dating your friend because you and I aren't together. I honestly wouldn't even call us friends. You run every time you see me. You wouldn't even talk to me without us being in a public place."

Ella was starting to get that creeping feeling of doubt again, like maybe she had been making this up the entire time. She had to ask about the one thing that still kept her up at night.

"Well, what about the video?" she searched him for a reaction, anything. A slight smirk, a flash of fear, but all she got was confusion.

"What video?" he asked.

She tried to hold back the feeling that she was losing it. "The video. Of you watching me sleep. You sent it to me about a month ago."

"Look, Ella I have no idea what video you're talking about but that sounds creepy as hell."

Ella wasn't sure how to respond. She'd been so convinced that Chad had sent her that video she hadn't considered that maybe someone else had broken in and done it. Maybe she was wrong and it wasn't from when she was with Chad at all. "I don't believe you," she said, still unable to consider accepting that it was anyone except him.

"Ok, well can I see it at least? So I know what I'm being accused of?" They were passing a little bistro where people were enjoying brunch. "Look, let's go in here and get something to eat. I'm starving."

"I didn't bring my wallet and I'm poor," Ella said, blurting out the first excuse that came to her mind.

"I'll pay," Chad said, already walking inside.

64

The host sat them at a booth, which Ella was grateful for so they each very clearly had their own side of the table. Once their server had taken their drink orders and left, Chad started in about the video again.

"Now will you let me see the video?" he asked eagerly.

Ella was apprehensive but reluctantly pulled out the phone, scrolled to the text from the unknown number and clicked on it. "Here. You can see it's from a weird number. Tap on the video."

Chad took the phone and watched the video. "Wow, I can see why you are creeped out, but I definitely didn't send this."

"You can say that all you want but who else could it have been?" Ella asked, still trying to fight off the musing that maybe it hadn't been him.

"Because it wasn't. Look," he paused the video and showed her a calendar on the wall in the background of the frame. It was a weekend he'd been out of town for business. Ella was floored. How had she missed this detail?

"I... "she couldn't find anything else to say. She just stared in disbelief and then looked at Chad, the face that had been haunting her. She started breathing hard. A little too hard. She realized she was hyperventilating.

Chad set her phone on the table and instructed, "El, breathe in for 1, 2, 3, 4. Then exhale for 1, 2, 3, 4. C'mon, let's take some deep breaths." He started breathing along with her, and she was mortified, thinking people were staring at her, even though she was sure that wasn't the case. It was just her anxiety taking over again. She calmed down a bit but felt like she needed to not be near Chad for a minute so she could catch her breath. Chad, who, was it possible that she'd been wrong about him all along? That he was just a sad, lonely guy who loved her?

"Excuse me," she said as she got up and went to the bathroom. She splashed her face with water and took deep breaths for a few more minutes. She was thankful no one had knocked on the door while she was in there, or that surely would have triggered her anxiety all over again.

With one final deep breath, she steeled herself and went back out to the table. Their drinks were sitting on the table, two waters, a 7Up for Chad and an orange juice for Ella.

"You feel better?" Chad asked.

"Yes, thank you." she answered, not sure if she should just be honest with how she felt right now, or do her best to keep up this emotional barrier she had erected between them. "Look, I'm sorry for thinking that was you. I'm sorry for thinking that you were being malicious this whole time. I'm just really sorry.

A sympathetic smile spread across his face. "El, you don't have to apologize to me for anything. We had a bad breakup. These things happen."

She nodded in thanks and took a drink of her orange juice. "You know what would be great with this? Some champagne," she laughed.

"Already ordered a flute. It's on the way," he said.

"Thank you." Ella wasn't sure how to process the feelings she had right now. Apparently, all of her friends had been right about him this whole time. What did that say about *her*, she wondered?

"Now, let's talk about this video. Have you gone to the police?"

"There's nothing they can do," she said, not wanting to go into the details of why.

"Hmm, well maybe we can try to look up this number it was sent from."

"Tried that too. No results."

Chad sat thinking for a minute. "Maybe you should consider getting some security cameras then."

"They're on their way," Ella said.

Chad smiled, "Maybe you didn't need me to look after you for all of that time after all."

That comment made Ella uneasy, him somehow insinuating that she needed his help.

The server arrived with her champagne and a tray of pastries.

Ella poured the champagne in her orange juice, took a sip, and that was the last thing she remembered before waking up tied to a chair in Chad's apartment.

65

Ella looked around. Chad's apartment was neat and tidy like it always was when they'd lived together, but it was almost hard to see through the pounding pain in her head. It was like every heartbeat caused a flash of light in front of her eyes. She tried to lift her hand to rub her forehead but found that both of her hands were tied behind her back. She tried to stand but her legs were tied to the chair legs. She was trapped.

"There you are!" Chad said, in his sickly sweet babytalk tone she'd known so well and somehow pushed to the back of her mind.

"What the fuck, Chad! What are you doing to me? How did I get here?" she yelled.

"Well, you had a little too much champagne earlier and got sloppy. But that's normal for you, right? So I had to help you out of the restaurant, and I brought you back up here."

"But I only had one glass."

"Yes, but I slipped a little something into your orange juice when you weren't looking," he said with a smirk that made her blood run cold.

"Why? What do you want from me?"

"I want you to *appreciate* everything I did for you," Chad said in an angry voice Ella couldn't remember hearing before. "I did so much for you, and you repaid me by breaking my heart and getting a restraining order? That wasn't very nice, Ella."

Ella wasn't sure if she should play along with his game or show him how she really felt. She knew he just wanted her affection, so she chose the former. "I'm so sorry I did that, Chad. I really am." The words felt like they burned her tongue as she said them, but it worked. He stopped pacing and looked at her.

"What?" he asked, obviously thinking it would be harder to get her to this point than he was proving to be.

"I'm sorry I treated you the way that I did. You didn't deserve that," she could tell she was getting through to him. He sat down on the chair across from her.

"Do you mean that?" he was skeptical.

"Yes!" she worried that she sounded more desperate than sincere. "Yes. You helped me see things as they really were today." He was quiet. "Look, why don't you untie me and we can continue our conversation about this. *About us.* I want your help." she tried to appeal to his desire to protect her.

"My help to what?"

"Your help to what?"

"To help me find who sent that video!"

"Oh, that. Well, I guess there was one little lie I told you," Chad looked apologetic. "I did take that video. I sent it to you from a burner phone."

"But you said you were out of town? The calendar…"

"I edited that before I sent it to you. I didn't realize it would be so easy to get you to remember. I thought I'd have to show you travel receipts or something, which I have, even though I never actually used them. I just wanted to make sure you hadn't found a way to get the police to take it seriously. It wouldn't be hard for a junior IT person to figure it out, but I knew you never would. I needed you to be scared by that so you'd let me protect you again."

Ella was holding back a flood of emotions. Fear, anxiety, but the strongest of them all was anger. She was so angry that she almost couldn't bear to keep faking that she sympathized with him. She swallowed hard.

"Well, I can see why you'd do that," feeling almost out-of-body at the effort it took her to stay calm and say this to him. He was apparently shocked too.

"You do?"

"Yes, of course. Like I said before, I'd mistreated you all of that time. And you just wanted me to see how much you were doing for me. You wanted me to love and appreciate you."

"Yes! That's exactly it. Now you understand." He rushed over and took her head in his hands. He looked into her eyes like he was going to kiss her, but instead he put a chemical-smelling cloth over her mouth, and she passed out.

66

Ella woke up again with a splitting headache. She was still in the same place in Chad's apartment, but this time she had tape over her mouth so she couldn't make a sound. The small amount of light coming in from the window made her think it was the next day, but she couldn't be sure how much time had passed.

Chad was nowhere to be seen, and there were boxes and suitcases everywhere. He was clearly packing up and getting ready to leave. Then she saw a wheelchair in the corner and got a rotten feeling in the pit of her stomach. She looked around again and sat very still, listening for any sign of movement within the apartment.

There was only silence. She couldn't scream so her best chance to be found was to get to the front door and bang on it. Using her bodyweight, Ella slowly moved the chair across the floor, one inch at a time. She kept listening to see if Chad was in the apartment but there was no sound.

Finally, she was within a foot of the door. Her plan was to put her back to the door so she could bang on it with her head and hopefully maneuver the chair to block him from coming inside as well. She was almost there when she heard the key in the lock and saw Chad standing there. He looked surprised and smiled down at her.

"Look who woke up," he said, weaving his way in and closing the door behind him. He dragged Ella back to the middle of the room. "I was downstairs in your apartment looking for this," he held up her passport, and Ella pushed down the anxiety attack she could feel coming on. "You see, we're moving. We're leaving the country and going where no one will look for us. I've even got this little wheelchair here for you so you don't have to wake up until we're there."

Ella fought against the bindings on her wrists until she felt blood dripping down her fingers. The slick wetness helped give her a little more wiggle room, but it was too late. Chad had seen her struggling and walked back over to her with the cloth. She was knocked out cold in a matter of seconds.

When she woke up this time, there were no boxes left in the apartment. Just the wheelchair and a suitcase. Chad was in the kitchen and Ella could hear the faucet running. He walked over to her. With the glass and a pill in his hand.

"Ok, you're going to need to do this one last thing. Take this pill and when you wake up we'll be together forever. You won't have to worry about anything. I'll take care of you and make sure you're safe." He went over and tried to remove the gag from her mouth and she bit him. "C'mon, Ella. Don't be like this. I don't want to force you to swallow this, but I will." He seemed in a rush now. His whole demeanor was more tense and she wondered why.

If it was in fact the next day, she'd have been expected at her new job, and when she didn't turn up, they'd call Mindy or someone, right? It was the only hope she had. She had to stall for as long as possible.

Chad walked back towards her. "Be nice this time, he growled."

With the gag off, Ella took a chance. "Wait! I'll take the pill, but I just want to know why you're doing this. Why can't you just trust me to go with you?"

"Well, you just bit me. So it's safe to say you're not exactly cooperative." He had a point. "But if you'll take this pill without giving me any trouble then you'll start to get some of my trust back."

She couldn't think fast enough with the drugs still in her system and her head throbbing. He slipped the pill in her mouth and started pouring water down her throat. She felt helpless and started choking when there was suddenly a knock at the door. Without thinking, Ella screamed through her coughs, "HELP! HELP ME!" She was able to cough up the pill, barely keeping it from sliding down her throat.

The knocking became stronger, a clear attempt to break down the door. Chad panicked. He looked to the window, and to the empty kitchen. He finally did the only thing he could and got Ella in a chokehold right as the door opened, and Zora, Trix, Mindy, Lulu, and three police officers barged in.

67

It took too long to choke a person, so without an instantly
deadly weapon like a gun or a knife, the officers had no
problem taking down Chad. Zora untied Ella who was
sobbing with relief. Trix walked over to Chad and slapped
him in the face. Mindy was on her phone with someone, and
Ella could hear her say, "Either she stays with us or we're
done. I'm coming home with her. Pack up and leave if you
want. I don't care." Lulu was standing off to the side, looking
out of place as usual.

"How did you know where to find me?" Ella was finally able
to say.

"When you didn't show up for work, Spencer called me. I
thought that was weird, so I texted you and the group chat.
When you never answered, we all started worrying."

"Then I remembered Chad had been asking me all kinds of
weird questions about you the last time we hung out, so I
broke up with him. But when you didn't answer, I thought it
was weird," Trix added.

"I used the spare key you gave me and checked on your apartment," Zora added. "You weren't there, but your room had papers lying everywhere and your car was still on the street. So I called the cops and had everyone come here. I stood outside of Chad's apartment and listened but thought that since I couldn't hear anything it might be best to let the muscle arrive before doing anything," she motioned to the cops.

"We were so worried," Lulu chimed in, and for once she didn't look like she hated Ella.

A police officer walked over to them. "Ma'am, we'd like to take you to the hospital to get checked out and gather any evidence," he motioned to the scabbed over rope burns on her hands.

"Ok, but 'I'm going with her and then she's coming home with me," Mindy said, standing in front of Ella like she was her guard dog.

"Are you sure?" Ella asked.

"Yes! I am so sorry for how I've acted lately." She turned to the rest of the women. "I'm sorry to all of you. I let a Creel override my better judgement. Never again!"

"Thanks, Min" Ella said as she followed the cop outside. She hadn't seen what happened to Chad after Trix slapped him, but now she saw him in the back of a police car. He smiled at her before the car drove away.

Epilogue

Chad got a 10-year sentence for kidnapping but was out in five with good behavior. Trix had been waiting for this day. She called up one of her friends. "I need a favor. Come to the club tonight."

A man in sunglasses and a dark coat walked into the club. Trix pulled him aside for a lap dance.

"I need you to kill a guy that just got out of prison, but I need it to look like a suicide."

"Is he a bad guy or is this some love thing?"

"Both. He's obsessed with my friend. He was in jail for kidnapping her and he'll start stalking her again now that he's out. The cops won't do anything, so I only see one way to deal with this."

"Sounds like a bad guy to me."

"Thanks," Trix smiled at him. She reached into the thigh-high boot she was wearing and pulled out a little pistol. "Do it with this. It's stolen. I bought it back when my friend was first scared of him. I don't need it anymore."

The man looked at her curiously.

"It's stolen," she said. "It'll look like he stole it and killed himself. No one will know."

"You make my job easy," he said, softening.

Trix finished her dance and he left.

A few days later, Trix was looking through the paper like she always did in the morning. A few pages back she saw a small article, only a few hundred words, with a picture of a car. The headline read, "MAN FOUND DEAD IN HIS CAR"

She read on. "A man identified as Chad Miller died of a gunshot wound to the head in a vacant parking lot downtown. The police believe the wound was self-inflicted with an unregistered gun that he purchased illegally. Chad was recently released from prison for a kidnapping sentence."

Trix smiled, knowing that no one besides she and the hitman would know the truth, but she was happy to know everyone was a little safer without Chad out there slinking around.

Note from the author

Thank you so much for reading *Attack*. I hope you had as much fun reading it as I did writing it. Ever since I was child, I've loved telling stories, and readers make that dream possible.

Time is the one resource we'll never get back, and I know that when you're reading you're investing your time in me and my story. I am very grateful for and humbled by that.

Attack started as me frantically writing a story to distract myself from an anxiety attack I was having at the moment. But then I built the characters and it turned into a story that a lot of us can relate with on some thematic level.

If you're interested in reading my other books and content, you can find me at nataliesaar.com or @nataliesaar on both Instagram and Twitter.

Sending you health, peace, and happiness.